CW01263290

THE TWELVE HOLIDATES

❄

EMMA ST. CLAIR

To Rob, for always begging me to read my books to you… even when I don't.

I really like you right now. <3

Copyright © 2020 by Emma St. Clair

All rights reserved.

No part of this book may be reproduced in any form or by any electronic or mechanical means, including information storage and retrieval systems, without written permission from the author, except for the use of brief quotations in a book review.

For information or permissions, contact: emma@emmastclair.com

Cover by Emma St. Clair

Proofreading by Devon Banta

This book is a novella in the Love Clichés series. It can be read as a standalone, but works best read right between *Falling for Your Fake Fiancé* and *Falling for Your Best Friend*.

DEAR DR. LOVE

From: FriendZoned@DrLove.advice
To: DrLove@DrLove.advice

Dear Dr. Love,
 I've been in love with my best friend since we were thirteen. The problem is that she has no idea.
 She kissed me one time, back in middle school. And I was so shocked, so excited, so *thirteen* ... that I didn't say anything.
 She took that to mean I must not like her back. Being a beacon of maturity, I didn't know how to tell her the opposite was true. But she stuck me permanently in the friend zone, which is where I've lived ever since.
 I don't think I can take watching her date losers and have her heart broken anymore. But I don't want to ruin over ten years of friendship. I can't lose her.
 What do I do?
 Sincerely,
 Friendzoned

From: DrLove@DrLove.advice
To: FriendZoned@DrLove.advice

Dear Friendzoned,

Your mission, should you choose to accept it, is to channel the bravery your bestie had when she kissed you way back then.

She put herself out there, while probably more terrified than you are right now, and just went for it.

It's time for you to do the same. Ideally, before a guy who's NOT a loser stakes his claim.

Go get her, cowboy!

-Dr. Love

DATE 1

❄

Taylor

I HAVE to wonder if the blogger who suggested waiting inside a giant stocking for your significant other actually tried it first. After spending thirty-one minutes waiting inside one for my boyfriend, I'm guessing no. Maybe it was one of those sponsored posts with a stocking brand, where they just HAD to write good things.

Because the post mentioned nothing about the heat inside of a giant stocking. This thing does NOT breathe. At. All.

Which means the cute holiday dress I'm wearing is now plastered to my body like a red velvet wetsuit. I also suspect that I smell, and not like the holiday cookie body spray I spritzed on before I climbed inside the stocking of doom.

My best friend, Weston, tried to warn me this was a bad

idea. But he's always a wet blanket when it comes to anything Chad related, so I've learned to tune him out.

Weston never thought we would last through the first year of Chad's law school, and just look at us now! Take that, Weston.

Assuming all goes well. Which is what I'm doing: hoping for the best. Chad says my optimism is one of my best qualities. That and my legs. They better be, considering how frequently I run.

How much longer is Chad going to take?

He was supposed to be here twenty minutes ago, based on his schedule. And one thing Chad and I have in common is that we do not deviate from our schedules. Maybe he stayed after work for drinks? But that's not like him. He should have been here seventeen minutes ago. I got here early just in case he did, and boy, am I regretting it now.

Finally, when I'm afraid I'm going to melt into a Christmas cookie scented puddle in the bottom of this knit monstrosity, I hear keys in the apartment door.

It's go time!

I straighten up, trying to retain the stocking's shape, which requires a tiny bit of contortionism and a whole lot of discomfort.

It will be worth it. It will. It has to be.

While the blog post focused on the sexytimes benefits of hiding yourself in the stocking, I'm thinking of it more in a symbolic way. (Which explains why I'm in a Christmas dress and not some kind of naughty Mrs. Claus nightie.)

I want Chad to see that I'm his. I'm all in. I mean, if waiting for him while he finished law school wasn't an indication enough, this should do the trick. I'm his, and I'm ready for phase two of our relationship.

He'll pass the bar and get a full-time job at Walker

Associates while I'll finally get the ring I've been patiently and not at all passive-aggressively waiting for. I'm not one of those pushy girlfriends who constantly hints about rings and timelines. No, I've just ... waited.

Anyway. Back to the present, Chad is here, and I'm about to show him that I'm really HIS. But tonight is just the start. This is the last week before Christmas, and the giant stocking is just one of twelve "holidates" I printed off from the blog post. The paper is a little bit damp after holding it in the stocking for thirty-one minutes, hopefully still readable. Once I've surprised him and am out of this literal sweat sock.

How long does it take the man to get his key in the lock?

Finally, the door opens. My heart beats faster. Come on, Chad. Get your cute butt in here!

The door slams, and I try not to let out a shriek of excitement. And just like when playing hide-and-seek as a kid, my eager nervousness might have resulted in a little loosening of the bladder region. I'm most definitely leaving an anonymous comment on the blog post after this. People need to know what they're getting into. Literally.

For some reason, Chad seems to have stalled out in the entryway. I hear shuffling, but no indication that his steps have moved any closer. His apartment isn't massive. I'm near the Christmas tree that I insisted Chad get the day after Thanksgiving.

Why is he just standing in the doorway?

My anticipation is on par with a five year old on Christmas Eve when she's hoping to get her first big-girl bike.

Finally, I hear Chad toss his keys in the bowl on the kitchen counter. Any second now ...

I hear a deep sigh—is this it?! Does he see me? I'm almost ready to squeal. Right about...

"Oh, *Chad*."

That sultry voice isn't part of the plan. Not my tonight plan. Not my anytime-ever plan.

It is very female, very breathy, and definitely going to ruin my holiday spirit.

A low growl follows, a sound which has to be coming from Chad, unless I'm somehow in another apartment. Or another dimension. I've certainly never heard him make THAT particular noise before.

My knees begin to tremble, and the paper list I've been clutching falls to the bottom of the stocking. The sounds continue.

Heavy breathing. A giggle. Rustling. They're getting closer, shuffling steps headed toward the couch. I feel a little more nauseated with each sound, and my humiliation grows.

Is this really happening?

And how do I extricate myself from this stocking of death before things in the room go too far?

How far, exactly, will they go?

I don't want to know the answer to that question, which is why I make the snap decision to make a run for the door.

Only, this is a bit tricky considering my hiding spot in plain sight in the stocking.

I try to step out of the stocking, averting my eyes so I don't have to see things I can't unsee. But I'm standing too close to the tree, and my heel catches on the string of Christmas lights. Lights I so carefully hung while Chad checked texts on his phone that he said were Very Important and School Related. Yeah, right.

The moment I realize my heel is tangled in the lights is the one where I see Chad and *her*, entwined on the couch, not unlike the way that Chad and I were two nights ago.

The sight makes me want to vomit. It would serve them

right if I did, and it's not out of the realm of possibility, especially considering the way I'm toppling toward them.

I stumble forward in an awkward step-hop, my heel still in the lights while the other is trapped in the stocking.

Their faces belong in a movie. The woman's wide blue eyes really are like the clichéd description of saucers. If saucers had spidery looking fake eyelashes attached to their edges, that is. And yeah, I'm judging her eyelashes. Isn't that my *right*?

Chad's face matches hers, the only difference being the shadow of regret I see in his eyes. Regret and ... is that pity?

Oh no. Not pity. Nope. Not taking that right now.

I'm going down. Right on top of them. There is no avoiding it. Spider-lashes opens her mouth even wider, if that's possible, since it already looks like she could fit her whole fist inside.

The amazing thing is how many thoughts have time to race through my head as I'm falling toward the couch.

I put my hands out to break my fall. My palms land right on spider-lashes' plump backside and then the tree lands on mine.

Then it's me and Chad and spider-lashes and the Christmas tree, all tangled on the couch together.

Not awkward at all.

With a pop and a shower of sparks, the string of lights goes out, and all I can think about is how Weston was right.

DATE 2

Weston

I SHOULD NEVER HAVE LET her go.

That's what I'm thinking as I open the door of my apartment to find Taylor in a wrinkled dress, clutching her heels in one hand and a person-sized Christmas stocking in her hand. The mascara tracks on her cheeks confirm what I already know: Chad is a total loser.

"He was cheating on me!" she says, throwing herself in my arms.

And as much as I want to throttle her idiot boyfriend—now *ex* boyfriend, I'm assuming—I can't be sad about getting to hold Taylor.

"Come on," I say, roughing a hand over her dark hair. I walk her to the couch where I've comforted her like this countless times before. It's THE couch. To Taylor, it probably doesn't mean much, but to me, it's a monument to my stupidity.

I shouldn't have let Taylor go. And I don't just mean to her stupid jerk of an ex's house to wait for him in a stocking. I should have cut that off at the start.

But I never should have let her go after she kissed me on this very couch when we were thirteen. That's what I'm thinking as I hold a sobbing, broken-hearted Taylor, wishing I was holding a happy, in-love-with-me Taylor instead.

I've gone over that pivotal moment so many times in my mind. Imagined me doing and saying all the right things instead of what I actually did.

We were in my parents' basement, watching *The Dark Knight* for probably the fiftieth time. Like most thirteen-year-old guys, I was obsessed with the new Batman franchise. And Taylor was equally as obsessed with Christian Bale, even if she didn't want to admit it.

I didn't see the kiss coming. Not even a little bit. My eyes were glued to the screen, watching Ra's Ah Ghul take on Bruce Wayne in his mansion. The dark moment before the light.

Looking back, I see what my idiot self then didn't. Taylor went to get a drink refill and plopped down on the couch much closer to me. Then she reached across me for the remote, and when her shoulder pressed into my scrawny chest, I'd angled my head to see the screen better.

Side note: it's no wonder I can so quickly peg every idiot Taylor dates. I'm working from experience here.

Anyway. When her subtle cues didn't take my eyes from the screen, Taylor went all in. She took my acne-dusted cheeks in her hands and pressed her mouth to mine, with all the enthusiasm and inexperience that a thirteen-year-old can.

And I ... didn't kiss her back.

I didn't move.

I was a hiker, coming across a mama bear and her cubs in the woods. Awestruck and terrified, I resorted to the third alternative in the fight or flight response—I *froze*.

It was the best moment of my life, one I'd dreamed about but had never imagined actually happening. I was stunned. Blown away. Lobotomized by that single, sweet kiss.

And when Taylor pulled away, searching my face for something, *anything*, all I gave her was the same look a big-mouthed bass does when it's on your line: wide eyes and a gaping mouth.

Taylor wisely chose flight, and high-tailed it down the street to her house. And that's where I made an even bigger mistake—I didn't go after her. I didn't call her. I didn't even walk over the next few days and ask her to hang out like I normally did that summer.

Because I had no idea what to do or say.

My feelings were simply too big for my little pea brain to handle. That kiss short-circuited my motherboard, blew all my fuses. If you've never been a teenage boy, you simply can't understand the Molotov cocktail it throws into your life. The feelings, the raging, hormones wreaking havoc on a confused physical body, all mixed with a maturity that's nonexistent.

Yeah, yeah. Excuses, excuses.

The thing was—I already had it bad for Taylor. I thought I'd shown her by the fact that I spent every waking minute with her, even when my other guy friends teased me mercilessly. I figured it was obvious. I had no idea she felt the same way until that kiss.

While I understand how my ineptitude came across as disinterest and maybe even dislike, it was the furthest thing from the truth. I was terrified. I couldn't work up the courage to go see Taylor, but I worked up a speech. Which was heavily influenced by Christopher Nolan movies and more fitting for a big budget action film, but whatever.

By that time, though, Taylor had spent two days convincing herself that I didn't feel the same way. She blew into my house with a smile like she always did, acting like nothing ever happened, except for the quick speech she made about how we were never to talk about that night again under pain of certain death and loss of friendship.

"You're my best friend, West," she'd said, "and that's all you'll ever be. Friends forever?" She'd even stuck out her hand for me to shake.

What was I supposed to do at thirteen? I had no game. Braces. A voice that cracked half the time I spoke. No knowledge of how girls worked, or that this was Taylor's way of protecting herself.

It felt like the worst kind of rejection.

So, with my stomach feeling like a garbage compactor crushing up all my insides, I shook her hand.

Leading me to this moment, where the douche of the day has just broken her heart again, and I'm the forever best friend left picking up the pieces of the woman I love.

"I supported him through law school," she sobs. "I gave up my dreams for him to succeed, because I thought I was doing it for *us*."

My T-shirt is soaked with her tears—and hopefully *just* tears—as she cries into my chest. Is it so terrible that a part of me eats this up because it means I get to hold her?

Yeah, it's terrible.

Because unlike the other jackholes that Taylor dated over the years, she was actually serious about Chad. To the point that she thought he was The One. It fills me with relief that he screwed this up so royally. But it also means that my girl is hurting. Bad.

All I can do is stroke her hair, let her soak my shirt with enough tears to stop a drought, and tell her she's going to be okay.

That's all I can do for *now*. Later? I'll exact my revenge, as I always do on her exes. But I'll plan that out another time.

"What did I do wrong?" Taylor pulls away to look up at me.

Her red-cheeked, tear-filled expression makes so much tenderness and protectiveness boil up inside me that it takes me a moment to locate words.

"Nothing, Tay. You did nothing wrong. Chad is the one who screwed up."

"Literally," she says, sniffling, and I wince at my careless word choice.

This is why I let Taylor do a lot of the talking. Whenever I do, I find ways to stick my size twelves right in my mouth.

"I'm sorry. What I meant was that Chad clearly didn't deserve you."

And he'll pay. Soon. Maybe I'll finally utilize the deer urine I've been stocking up on at the hunting store.

Taylor chuckles bitterly. "How many times have you said that now? At what point do I become the common factor in my failed relationships?"

"The only common factor is that you keep choosing ..." I search for a creative insult that adequately covers how awful her exes are. Nothing seems quite bad enough.

"Guys out of my league?" she offers.

"*No*." My voice is so low, so rough that Taylor startles a little. I take a breath, getting myself back under control. "The common factor is that *you* are too good for *them*."

Her tears have dried and Taylor is moving into the part of

recovery where she wants to dissect things. I hate seeing her cry, but the autopsy of her busted relationships? No, thank you. The last thing I want is to hear more about Chad.

Time to play offense.

"What's this?" I ask, pulling a crumpled and damp paper from her fist. I thought it was a tissue, though she seemed completely happy using my shirt instead.

"Don't look at that," Taylor says, trying to snatch it from my hands.

I can play this game. I *like* this game, because it involves touching Taylor, even if in a playful way. I'm a desperate man; I'll take the scraps that fall from the table.

Grabbing both of her wrists in my hand, I start to read what appears to be a printed list with a few notes scribbled in Taylor's handwriting.

"'The Twelve Holidates. Number one—dress in a life-sized stocking and wait for your significant other in their bedroom. Wearing something ... sexy.'"

If I needed another reminder to keep my mouth shut, here it is. I can't even breathe after reading the words on this paper.

Sexy?

It's like my brain tripped on that one word, and I can't manage to recover my balance. I know Taylor and Chad dated for two years. But as much as she and I tell each other about our lives, we don't *kiss* and tell.

I prefer to think that after our first kiss, Taylor's lips never touched anyone else's. She just did a lot of ... hand holding. Years and years of hand holding.

Realistic, I know.

My blood is somehow freezing and boiling at the same time, like I'm now a chemistry experiment gone awry. I have no right to feel possessive, to feel jealous, to feel angry.

Yet I am all of these things and more. I want so badly to be the man she wants. Why couldn't it be me? Why couldn't I have kissed her back all those years ago and kept her all this time?

Taylor jerks out of my grasp and curls into herself at the end of the couch, covering her face with her hands. I don't even realize that I've crumpled the list into a tiny ball until Taylor mutters something I can't quite hear.

"What?" I ask, smoothing the paper flat against my thigh.

"I wore this! Just a dress! Not anything ... weird. Or sexy."

What Taylor fails to understand is that she doesn't need to dress in something sexy to be sexy; she just *is*.

"I also waited in the living room, not his bedroom. Maybe that's the problem! I changed the list! I should have worn something sexy in the bedroom, just like they said."

"What? No. No. Definitely no."

Taylor grabs the list from my hand again and begins to scan the page. I take it right back with enough force that it rips slightly.

"No, you don't. Forget this list." I shove it under my leg to read later. "Forget Chad."

Taylor sighs. "I'm so embarrassed. How are you still friends with me? I'm like the hot mess to end all hot messes. What am I going to do with myself?"

She's got the hot part right. Even after she's been crying for hours, Taylor is the most beautiful woman I've ever seen. Always has been. It's not just her dark brown hair and eyes a blue that no sky color, wall color, or crayon color has ever matched.

Taylor's got that something, underneath all the outside stuff, like a glow that lights it all up. Her quirkiness, her sweetness, her unending optimism.

15

Despite what Taylor thinks, she's the furthest thing from a mess. Or she will be, once she recovers. That's what I need to focus on: helping her bounce back.

"What *we're* going to do is get you over Chad. Even his name sucks, Tay. I swear, it could be a curse word. 'That guy who cut me off in traffic is a total *Chad*. Don't be such a *Chad*.'"

The sound of Taylor's laughter smooths out the twisted-up feeling in my gut.

Take that, Chad. Did you ever make her laugh like that? Didn't think so.

"You're the best, Weston. How do you always know how to cheer me up?"

Because I actually pay attention. Because I know her better than anyone else in the world. Because I love her.

And suddenly, I have an idea so idiotic it just might work. Not just to cheer Taylor up. But one that might help me do what I should have done years ago—tell her how I really feel.

It goes along with the response I got from Dr. Love. Because I'm desperate enough that I emailed an advice columnist, who also happens to be Taylor's boss. I figured it couldn't hurt, and it's all anonymous, even Dr. Love's identity, which Taylor hasn't ever told me.

Dr. Love's advice? Man up and tell Taylor what I should have told her all those years ago.

The plan I've just come up with will do that. In a roundabout way, sure. But step by step, it will help lay the groundwork for me confessing my feelings.

Without even knowing it, Taylor just gave me a giant help.

I pull the list out from under my leg. "Speaking of cheering you up, I've got an idea to help you get over Chad. We're going to take this list of 'holidates'—cheesy name, by the way—and we're going to do everything on it. But better."

She's already shaking her head. "No. That's just going to remind me of how stupid I am."

"Chad's the stupid one. And he doesn't get to ruin this. Give me a pen. You've got one in that purse of yours, don't you?"

I know she does. Along with a mountain of receipts, a half-eaten Twix, and an extra pair of socks. Just in case. Her purse falls somewhere between a doomsday prep kit and a back-alley dumpster.

She hands me a pen. It's pink with a fuzzy ball on top. She shrugs. "It's the only one I have."

"Clearly, this was one of Chad's pens."

She's laughing again as I go to work on her list.

"First things first—you already did number one. Though"—I tap the pen on my lips—"you could put on something sexy and get in the stocking for me?"

Too far? That was too far.

Taylor is not moving, just staring at me with wide eyes. Note to self: ease her into this. Slowly.

"Kidding. Kidding. No more giant stockings."

Not this year, anyway. But if this plan works, is it too much to hope for one in the future? Adding it to my mental list ...

"I'm never getting in this thing again," Taylor says, kicking at the pile of fabric. "We should burn it. Yes! That's it! Cross off number one and put 'Burn giant stocking' there instead. Your apartment complex has an outdoor fire pit, right?"

"On it." I adjust the first date, then cross out part of the second. "And we're going to combine the ceremonial burning of the giant stocking with holidate number two: s'mores.

Roasted over the flames of the burning stocking rather than a campfire."

Taylor claps her hands. "I love s'mores!"

"I know! And I happen to have everything we need to make them right here."

Because I'm the kind of guy who stocks Taylor's favorite snacks. I tell myself that it's thoughtful, not depressing.

Taylor jumps up and begins dragging me by the arm toward the kitchen. "What are we waiting for? Let's get out there!"

And this is how I finally start trying to win over the woman I've loved for almost half my life.

Hopefully, date one isn't an indication of all the dates to come. Because, as we quickly realize, the fumes from burning synthetic fabric are basically a toxin, and will ruin marshmallows roasted over them.

So, dates one and two were a bust. But Taylor has moved from tears to laughter. My job isn't done, but it's a start.

Ten more holidates to go.

DATES 3 & 4

Taylor

"Someone's in a good mood today," Sam says.

We've made it almost all the way through Monday morning, usually one of our busiest days. Full of unpleasant meetings, talk of website hits and ad revenue and the kind of things that the writers (Sam) and lowly assistants (me) don't want to think about. But today, I may or may not have been humming and drumming out a beat on my desk while going through Sam's Dr. Love inbox. I guess I *am* in a good mood.

"Big date with Chad last night?" Sam asks.

"Ugh. No." My mood is definitely *not* thanks to Chad. "Chad and I broke up."

"Whoa! What happened?"

I wrinkle my nose, remembering the sting of humiliation from the night before. But it's quickly replaced by the memory of standing with Weston, watching the stocking go up in flames, melting into a pulpy mess. The smell was terrible, and it made our s'mores inedible. It was perfect.

I never would have imagined moving from devastation to sheer joy all in one night. But that's the Weston effect.

"Let's just say I wasn't the only woman in Chad's life," I tell Sam.

"No! You caught him cheating?"

I nod. "Literally. I had a front-row seat. Actually, better. It was the equivalent of having the exact spot on the water ride where you get completely drenched."

"You seem to be taking this remarkably well. What's your secret? Dr. Love could use some breakup tips."

That's the thing about working with Sam, whose public persona is Dr. Love. She's great with advice, but the tradeoff is that she's always hungry for stories she can use in the column or the book she's working on. Basically, everyone she knows becomes potential material for her to write about.

I don't really mind. She's been good to talk to, her advice often echoing what Weston says. Just thinking about Weston has me smiling again.

"How about I buy lunch and you spill?" Sam asks.

"I've actually got lunch plans, and I probably need to get going."

"A date? Already?"

I laugh, waving her off. "No. Not a date. Just hanging out with Weston. He's actually the reason for my good mood."

I fill Sam in on the events of the night before, starting with falling out of the stocking on top of Chad and spider-lashes, and ending with adapting the list of holidates with Weston.

Sam looks thoughtful. "I'm glad you're handling this so well. I mean, two years is a long time to be with someone and have it end like that. Not to rub it in. Sorry."

"It's okay." I shrug. "I should care more. Maybe I cried it all out. Or maybe burning the stocking was cathartic."

"Or maybe ..." Sam trails off, a smile tugging at her lips.

I know that look. It means she thinks she's figured something out. I have a feeling I know what she's thinking. But she's wrong. I cross my arms, waiting.

Her eyes meet mine. "I've heard you talk about Weston for years. He's your best friend, right?"

"Yes, and *just* a friend."

"Hm. Are you sure?"

I'm used to this question. From my parents, from my friends, and in the eyes of his few girlfriends who lasted long enough to meet me.

"Guys and girls *can* be friends, you know. It happens."

"Only if there's no attraction either way," Sam says. "Otherwise, it's usually friendship with some hopefulness attached to it."

I swallow hard. It's easy to say that Weston and I are just friends. It's harder to say that I'm not attracted to him. I'd be crazy not to notice how handsome my best friend is. Tall and broad-shouldered with caramel eyes and dark hair. I even like his beard, which is just the right length for kissing without giving your face an unwanted microdermabrasion. NOT that I've thought about kissing him. (I totally have.)

Add his thoughtfulness, sense of fun, and quirky sense of humor, and Weston is a catch some girl should have snapped up already.

I gave up the dream of that girl being me years ago.

"Nope. No attraction."

"Really? Huh." She looks thoughtful. "Guess I was wrong."

Sam is dangling bait in front of me. I know it's bait, but I still can't resist nibbling.

"Wrong about what?"

Shifting on her desk perch, Sam steeples her fingers. "I just always got the sense when you talked about Weston that you had feelings. Or maybe he did."

"*He* definitely doesn't."

The words leave my mouth before I realize what I've actually revealed. Something I've always known—that my feelings never died for Weston. Just as I've known he doesn't feel the same way about me.

"But you do?"

"It doesn't matter," I tell Sam. "Long ago, we decided to be just friends. He made it VERY clear that he didn't want more. Embarrassingly clear."

The burn from Chad's unfaithfulness has already lessened, but the rejection at age thirteen has not dulled. I cannot think about that moment where I laid it all on the line for Weston without feeling it deep in my gut. The shame, the rejection, and the disappointment never lessened, all these years later.

I've also never stopped wondering what would have happened if he kissed me back. Or, if I'd waited a few years, when I wasn't so awkward and I had some actual experience with kissing. Maybe he would have responded. He might have loved me like I loved him.

Liked, I remind myself. *You* liked *him. Past tense. And definitely not love.*

"But you're going through the list of holiday dates with Weston? As ... friends?"

"Yep. He suggested it as a way to help me forget about Chad."

"*He* suggested it? Interesting."

"It's just for fun. That's actually why I have lunch plans."

"What's today's date?"

I grab my bag and slip on my heels, which I'd replaced with the fuzzy slippers I keep under my desk. "We're getting photos with Santa."

Sam laughs. "The mall Santa?"

"I guess. I didn't ask. West set it up. It's funny. I don't know what I was thinking. Chad would never have done any of these things with me."

"Good thing you've got Weston."

I can hear the tone in Sam's voice. "As *friends*," I say.

She holds up both hands. "I didn't say anything. Have fun with St. Nick. And your good buddy."

"I will," I say, knowing that I'll have a blast.

Even though Sam's questions have me thinking, for the first time in a long time, about possibilities I stopped considering years ago with Weston. I probably shouldn't start thinking about them again now, wondering about what ifs.

But now that the door has cracked open, it's not going to be easy to close it again.

"Are you sure we should be doing this?" I whisper to Weston, glancing around the line at the sea of families, all of whom have little children.

He smirks. "Hey. It was your list."

I shove him lightly, remembering too late how solid he is. I basically bounce off. "I got the list from a blog. We should have burned it last night," I grumble.

"Aw, where's your sense of Christmas adventure?"

Weston gives the end of my hair a light tug, then lifts the strand to his nose. I swat him away.

"Did you change your shampoo?" he asks.

I flush, because *Weston noticed my shampoo??*

"I threw out the stuff Chad gave me. It was some kind of green tea organic something or other. Made my hair smell like dirty feet."

Weston snorts. "I like this. Smells more like *you*."

He takes another long sniff before stepping away. I try to tell my sprinting pulse that there's no cause for excitement. Weston has known me forever. Of course, he's familiar with the scent of my hair. That's normal for friends. Right? Sure.

I mean, I know West's scent. There isn't a name for it. It's partly that spicy, manly smell that some guys seem lucky enough to have seeping from their pores. Then there's his cologne, which I think must be the same one he's been wearing since junior high because he smells so familiar. So much like home.

"Keep the line moving," a woman calls out from behind us.

I hadn't realized people had started to move again. I turn and give her a smile as Weston and I move forward. "Sorry!"

She doesn't smile back. Neither do her twin girls, who I swear look like they're straight out of *The Shining*. I turn back around, grabbing Weston's arm in a vise grip.

"Whoa, cowgirl," Weston says. "Where's the fire?"

I shift closer to whisper, but he still has to lean down because he's so much taller than me. "Potential demon spawn behind us. Don't turn around."

Weston is laughing silently. I can feel him shaking against me. "What?"

"Twin girls from *The Shining* at our six. Don't look! They might steal your soul."

"You're not still watching horror movies, are you? You know you can't take it."

Not without someone to hold onto. And Chad never wanted to volunteer. Weston never minded.

"No way." I pause, and for just a moment, sadness overcomes me. "Chad loved war movies and documentaries. He said they were educational."

Weston makes a humming noise but doesn't say anything. He's probably sick of hearing about Chad. And all my exes. It seems like I'm always the one coming to him with my problems. His relationships tend to fizzle out before they get too far. Honestly, I can't be all that sad about it. I've hated every woman he dated on sight. Even before sight, in some cases. Just knowing he was dating someone was enough reason to hate them. Clearly, Weston didn't have that problem, because he's let me cry on his shoulder so many times. My chest feels tight at the thought.

"Are you still with me?" Weston knocks his shoulder into mine.

I give him a smile that's all on the surface. Because deep down, I'm feeling a creeping sadness. Maybe it's losing Chad. Or the way the Christmas season reminds me of the people who will be missing from our table this year. Like my grandma, who passed last March. And, of course, I won't have a date with me for the Christmas Eve party with Weston's and my families. I'll be alone. Again.

"Tay?" Weston's looking at me with concern.

"I'm here," I tell him.

"Good. Because this is supposed to be fun. Remember?"

I nod. Right. Fun. Because sitting on Santa's lap as a twenty-three-year-old is *fun*.

"West, maybe we should—"

"Next!" a voice calls. Too late to turn back now. A little boy is moving forward to sit on Santa's lap and now we're at the front of the line.

"Time to find out if you've been naughty or nice," Weston

teases, gently pushing me forward to the red velvet rope at the edge of the decorated workshop.

"I'm always nice," I protest.

"Mm-hm. Tell that to the man in red."

Suddenly, a blonde dressed in a red and white costume that looks like it's missing a few yards of fabric steps in front of us with a clipboard. Other than the elf ears under her red hat, her short skirt and tight sweater would look more fitting at a nightclub. Her bored expression shifts into something a lot more perky when she spots Weston behind me.

"Hi. I'm Brandi, Santa's elf helper." She ends with a giggle and a finger twirling her blonde hair, two things that I bet aren't part of her normal character. "Can I have your card?"

Weston leans forward to hand Brandi the card he filled out at the start of the line. She brushes her fingers over his hand as she does so, her grin brightening. I frown, taking a step closer to Weston.

Brandi scans the form, then looks up, her expression hopeful and fixed on Weston, like I'm not even standing here. I don't like it.

"Y'all aren't a couple? It says on the form you're friends."

I glance up at Weston. It's true; we are just friends. But somehow I feel betrayed knowing he wrote it down. Like now it's *official* official, immortalized on Santa's form forever in his own handwriting.

West gives me a look I can't read and then clears his throat. "We're uh …"

Brandi seems to be inching closer. *Sorry, elf-witch. Not today. Not on my watch.*

I wrap an arm around his waist. "*Very* close friends," I tell Brandi. "Very. Close."

She looks between the two of us, her eyes narrowing, assessing. I'm not sure how far I want to push this. Or why it even matters that this half-dressed she-elf is falling all over Weston.

It's not like I haven't seen it before. When Weston and I go places together, it's like he emits a supersonic signal irresistible to the female species. And yeah, it's always bothered me. Never so much as right now.

Brandi turns to help the family currently having their photo taken, and Weston looks down at me. I'm still clinging to him like a Christmas ornament in my red and green sweater covered in bells. We decided to combine dates, so today counts for a photo with Santa and an ugly Christmas sweater event. Weston picked mine out, and I think it might need to join the stocking in his fire pit.

A faint smile plays on his lips.

"*Very* good friends?" he says.

I've still got my arm around him and I find the spot on the side of his ribs that I know is ticklish. He laughs, trying to jerk out of my grip, but I don't let him go.

"We are very good friends," I say. "Aren't we?"

Weston's hand comes up to cover mine, stopping my tickle assault. But instead of letting go, he keeps his hand in place.

His caramel eyes meet mine, and for a few beats, all the sounds of the mall fade away. My hand is hot underneath his big palm, so, *so* hot. The heat travels to my wrist and up the sensitive skin on the inside of my elbow.

Weston and I have touched many times over the years, but has there ever been this thick tension between us? For once, I can't read the expression in his eyes. His stare is intense, like he's trying to tell me something.

Does he feel this too? Could Weston possibly—

"Your turn, *friends*."

Brandi interrupts our moment and the question I'm not

sure I'm ready to ask. Because I don't know that I could stand putting myself out there one more time for Weston. It hurt too badly the first time. He's had years—*years*—to make a move, and he never has.

That tells me all I need to know.

I pull away, wanting to put space between us. But of course, that leaves an opening for Brandi, who slips her arm through his, leading him over to Santa's seat with a big smile on her face.

"Such a Chad," I mutter.

I didn't think I said it loudly enough for Weston to hear, but he barks out a laugh as he extricates himself from Brandi's clutches. I toss a glare her way, and she slinks back to her post at the edge of the workshop.

"Ho ho ho! What big kids we have here. Who's going to sit on Santa's lap?"

Weston and I exchange glances. Dumb as it may sound, we didn't talk about the logistics of this. Now it seems awkward and borderline inappropriate.

"Not it," we say at the same time. And then, "Jinx."

Reverting back to a game we played incessantly as kids makes all the tension from the last few minutes, good and bad, slip away like a skin I've shed. Weston raises his brows and I raise mine right back. He shrugs, and I shrug.

Santa coughs, probably trying to get our attention, but it quickly dissolves into what sounds like a smoker's cough, thick and wheezy. I do my best to laugh silently, because until Weston and I buy each other sodas, the jinx is in full effect. Unless one of us breaks, which ups the ante to buying dinner for the other person.

"Well? We've got children waiting," says Santa, as Weston's shoulders silently shake.

The glow of laughter lights his eyes, shifting them to a

warm, golden brown. I could stare into his eyes forever and never tire of the color.

The smile slowly slips from my face as the full weight of that thought hits me like a battering ram.

Suddenly, Santa's lap doesn't seem so bad. I plop down unceremoniously, perhaps a bit harder than I should, based on the grunt he lets out. Weston, fully committed to this silent game we're playing, mirrors me, settling down on Santa's other knee, also with more force than intended.

"Oh—ho ho," Santa says, coughing again, so hard this time that his belly—which is obviously very real, by the way—jiggles against both our backs. His knees tremble, jostling me and Weston toward one another. I almost lose my seat, grabbing West's arm for balance and grinning like a fool.

This is going to be some picture, I think, just before the flash starts popping.

And it is. When we walk away, holding up the hastily printed picture, we both look half-crazed with gleaming eyes and smiles bigger than Christmas morning. My hand is clutching Weston's sleeve, and in the ugly Christmas sweaters we're wearing, the photo looks even more ridiculous. I want to frame it and put it on my mantle.

As soon as we leave Santa's workshop, Weston tugs my arm, pointing toward an alcove with restrooms and a vending machine.

To some, this whole jinx thing might be stupid. Well. It is stupid. But it's *our* stupid thing, and we're both too stubborn to let it go. Our silence lasts until I dig enough change from the bottom of my purse to supply us both with sodas. He hands me a Dr. Pepper, and I hand him a Sprite. How he still manages to drink such a boring soda, I'll never know.

Our silence lasts until we each take a sip, and then our laughter sputters out, loud and raucous, drawing attention from a mom with a stroller. She gives us both disapproving glares, like we're doing something more than laughing in a hallway.

I understand her impulse though, because this moment feels like more to me too. Only, I can't seem to turn away, and I definitely don't want to.

DATE 5

Weston

THE NEXT DAY in my office, I answer my cell phone without even looking. That's how deep I am into planning the remaining holidates with Taylor, even though I should be looking at spreadsheets and balancing the year-end sales totals.

If I had looked at my phone, I would have seen YOUR DEAR MOTHER, a customization Mom added, and let it go to voicemail. Not because I'm avoiding my mom or anything, but because if I answered every time she called, we would basically talk at all times.

"Weston! You answered! I've been trying to reach you!"

I make a last note on the margin to call the skating rink and then drop my pen. Talking with my mother requires my full attention so I don't accidentally agree to go caroling or be in charge of the turkey fryer for our famous Christmas Eve dinner.

"Hey, Mom. How's it going?"

"You'd know if you listened to the seven voicemails I've left you."

"Mom, that's excessive. Even for you. I'm assuming no one died or you wouldn't sound so excited."

"Unfortunately, Uncle Tony is still hanging on."

Uncle Tony is our dog, an irrationally mean and completely blind Pekingese. Mom can't bring herself to have him put down, so we've been waiting for him to die for four years. He's basically the only reason I've had to buy any new pants since college. Once he latches on, it's bye-bye to your cuffs.

"And Grandma is coming to dinner this year."

I groan. "I thought we agreed that we would visit the home on Christmas Day, but that we weren't letting her out."

If I sound cold, it's because Grandma is basically the human version of Uncle Tony. Except what she latches onto with her dentures is your soul.

"I know, but she insisted. I guess they printed up the menu for Christmas Eve dinner at the home, and she refuses to attend a dinner where yams are served."

"Yams? We have to spend Christmas Eve dinner with Grandma because of *yams*?!"

In our family, Christmas Eve is the big event. We have a huge meal, open presents, and attempt to drink our weight in eggnog. It used to be a neighborhood thing, but so many families have moved over the years that now it's just our family and Taylor's.

And this year, I was hoping to finally be able to announce that Taylor and I are a couple. Throwing Grandma into the mix will make things ... interesting. While it's no secret that my mom and Taylor's mom have been hoping Tay and I would end up together, Grandma hates her. Which only means good things for Taylor. If Grandma does like someone, it calls their whole character into question.

"Maybe we should serve yams," I suggest.

"Oh, Weston. Don't be such a baby. It's your *grandmother*."

"Are you sure? Because the last time she attended Christmas Eve dinner, she told me I must be adopted because there's no way she was related to someone with a hipster beard."

"Grandma knows about hipsters?"

"Grandma knows *everything*."

Mom is silent for a moment. "Well. Maybe we'll get her started early on the eggnog."

"She's worse when she drinks."

"Maybe we can give her a job to do, like making one of the side dishes."

"Do you trust her not to put laxatives in our food?"

"Probably." But Mom doesn't sound so sure. "Maybe we *will* have yams."

"That's the spirit," I say.

"Anyway, you've distracted me from the real reason I'm calling. I met someone!"

I know we aren't doing a video chat, but I still pull the phone away from my ear and look at it.

"Mom? Is there something you and Dad forgot to tell me?"

Like, maybe, that you've secretly gotten divorced or are now swingers?

"Not for me, silly. Which you'd know, by the way, if you listened to your voicemails. I met someone for *you*."

"Ohhhh. How … interesting." And poorly timed, considering my end game for the week.

But it's not like I can tell Mom my plans. She'd much rather I date Taylor than whatever woman she's met for me. If I spill the beans now, Mom will go completely bananas. We're talking tears, yard signs announcing it, and a marching band. She'll call Taylor's mom, who will call Taylor, and then there go all my plans to win her over this week.

Plus, if I tell Mom about it, and then Taylor rejects me …

I swallow hard. I haven't given much thought to my plan *not* working. I'm afraid if I do, I'll chicken out altogether. Taylor will meet a good guy one of these days, and I'll spend the rest of my life full of regret.

Mom is still going on. "I know you hate being set up, but this woman is different."

"I was actually thinking about bringing someone this year," I say, which is somewhat true. It's just that Taylor will be there whether or not she's my date.

"She's a model!" Mom says. "Well. A *foot* model."

I cover my mouth to hide my laughter. A *foot* model. How did that even come up in their conversation? And where did Mom meet a foot model, anyway?

She's still going. "But her face is really nice too. She could just as easily be a face model. Or a leg model." Mom pauses. "All her parts are really nice."

"Her *parts*?" No sense hiding my laughter now. "Are we at an FFA meeting talking about a prize sheep?"

"Stop it. You know what I mean. And even if you bring someone, Gisele will be there so you can keep your options open."

"The foot model's name is Gisele?" I ask.

"Unique name, isn't it? I think she's from Europe. She has an accent."

"Is she married to a pro football player by any chance?"

"Of course not! I wouldn't set you up with someone who's married!"

I clear my throat. "Right. Just had to make sure it wasn't another model named Gisele."

"You know another model named Gisele? What a small world!"

Indeed.

Mom continues. "I know you don't like being set up, but I'm so tired of watching you mope and pine after Taylor every year. Especially since she's with Chad."

I could correct her. I should correct her. But talking about Taylor right now is like navigating a minefield. The wrong tone of voice or choice of words, and BOOM! Mom will know everything.

Instead, I choose sarcasm. "If you meet any other single women this week, be sure to invite them as well. It can be like my own personal version of *The Bachelor*. We'll let Grandma be the judge."

Rather than laughing at my obvious joke, Mom sounds thoughtful when she says, "My barista this morning said she was single. Maybe I could ask her."

I twirl a pen between my fingers. "How are her feet? I have very high foot standards. If she couldn't model them, I'm not interested."

"I'll ask to see them tomorrow when I get my morning mocha!"

"I was just kidding. Mom, do *not* ask the barista if you can see her feet. And please don't invite anyone else. If you could uninvite Gisele, that would be great."

"See you Friday!"

"Mom!"

But she's already disconnected the call. Christmas Eve is

going to be quite the party. I wonder if I should just skip ahead and tell Taylor how I feel, the way I should have done years ago. Maybe I don't need to go through all these dates to work up the courage or win her over. It's not like I'm a stranger. She already knows me better than anyone else.

But she knows me as a *friend*. I need her to realize we could be more.

So, it's back to the plans I go, trying to make sure each of these holidays—still a terrible name—helps ease Taylor into seeing me as more than just her best friend.

HER FACE as we park outside the rink does not inspire confidence. "Weston, this isn't ice skating."

"Nope." I grin at Taylor, then tug her hand to pull her out of my car. "Come on. Ice skating is *so* last year. This will be much more fun."

She's shaking her head, but takes my hand as I help her out of the car. Our hands linger together for a moment, and the feeling of her warm fingers in mine makes me happier than such a small gesture should.

Until she blinks hard, as though clearing her head, and stuffs her hands in her coat pockets. "Guess I won't need my jacket. Or hat. Or scarf."

"Probably not. But on the plus side, the snack bar has hot cocoa."

"Really?"

"I called to check."

It also has snow cones, another Taylor favorite. Honestly, I probably could have replaced all twelve dates with sugary treats and done just as well.

As soon as we step inside the roller rink, it's clear why all the romantic holiday movies choose ice skating for their romantic dates. The scent of wood, feet, and the faint aroma of body odor hit us just before the lights from the disco ball do. Romantic, it is not. Though the teenage couple making out by the snack bar didn't get the memo.

"Wow," Taylor says slowly. "This is …"

"Going to be fun. Don't fight it, Tay. They're playing our song."

Taylor tilts her head to the side, listening, before she begins to laugh. And laugh.

"This is One Direction. And we don't have a song."

I lean closer, my lips barely brushing her ear. "Time to remedy that. Come on."

I turn away, my heart thumping out an erratic rhythm after having my lips so close to her skin. My plan is to incrementally increase our physical contact, like I'm slowly turning up the volume knob, hoping the attraction goes both ways.

I can't tell if my whisper in her ear had the same effect as it did on me, but it takes her a moment to catch up to me at the skate rental counter. When she smiles at me, her cheeks are pink, and I'll take that as a good sign. A few minutes later, we're both attempting to lace up brown and orange skates that have seen better days … in the 1980's.

I get to my feet unsteadily and Taylor joins me, grabbing my arm as she finds her balance. Neither of us are good at skating, on blades or wheels, so I thought falling on a wooden rink would be better than a wet, icy one.

The trade-off is that instead of a romantic Christmas tradition under the stars, we've got pop music from ten and twenty years ago, a slew of small children to avoid, and a few older kids who clearly spend way too much time in here based on their skill level.

Taylor and I can barely make it around the rink. My feet weigh a hundred pounds and the wheels need a few good sprays of WD-40. On the plus side? Every time Taylor starts to fall, she grabs my arm.

Lots of touching? Check.

Laughter? Check.

Romance? Meh. We'll see. I'm not sure if it's the overall smell of the place or the fact that just staying upright takes so much of our concentration, but so far, this date definitely lands on the friendly side of things. And I need to move it toward the romantic side, ASAP.

Taylor pauses by the rink exit, using the wall to keep from falling over. "I've got to go to the bathroom. And maybe get some water. Are you ready for a break?"

"I'll snag some for us at the snack bar. Hot cocoa?"

She wrinkles her nose. "I'm too sweaty. Just water, please."

"One water coming right up."

But as soon as she's out of sight, I skip the snack bar and stop by the DJ booth. Correction: I fall *into* the DJ booth on my way to the snack bar.

"I'm so sorry," I say, trying unsuccessfully to get back up.

"It's not the first time, man," the DJ says, helping me untangle my skates from the cords underneath his chair.

When I'm free and back upright, I grab the low wall by the sound equipment to avoid any further accidents.

"I was hoping you can do me a favor. Did you see the girl I was skating with?"

He smirks. "I saw you with a girl. Not sure 'skating' is the right word for what you were doing. Kidding, man."

I shake my head, smiling sheepishly. "Yeah, we suck. I wondered if you could do a couples skate when we get back out on the floor."

He holds up his hand for a high five. "My man! Making a move at the skating rink. Old school. Any particular song?"

I think back through songs I remember listening to with Taylor in my car or hers, or even at school dances. Nothing comes to mind.

He pats me on the shoulder. "How about you trust me to give you something romantic?"

"Sounds good. Thanks, man."

A few minutes later, Taylor makes it to the table where I'm seated with two waters and a rainbow snow cone. Her eyes light up.

"I love snow cones!"

"I know."

I can't help but watch Taylor's mouth as she eats. What a lucky, lucky spoon.

"What color is my tongue?" Taylor asks, sticking her tongue out.

I grin. "Purple."

"Want some?"

Taylor holds the spoon out for me. Without breaking eye contact, I open my mouth. Somehow, eating a snow cone in the snack bar of a skating rink is *not* friendly, and I couldn't be happier about it.

Taylor watches the spoon disappear between my lips, and I grab her wrist as she starts to pull away. The air between us thickens, just the way it did the day before. Or is it just me? Am I the only one who feels this electricity and the tension between us?

I don't think I am.

Taylor's eyes take on a glazed look. They move from my eyes back to my mouth. That's good, right?

And then a voice over the loudspeakers interrupts that thought.

"It's time for the couples' skate. Couples, make your way to the floor."

"Skate with me?" I ask, my voice low and rough.

Taylor nods. We make our way unsteadily to the floor, where the DJ has chosen "Just the Way You Are" by Bruno Mars. Not really a *slow* song, but it will do.

As we reach the edge of the rink, I hold out my hand. Taylor doesn't hesitate, sliding her palm into mine. As we link fingers and begin to skate, I try to keep my emotions in check. I'm walking a fine line. If I step out too far, the fall might kill me. If I don't step out enough ... I might never get my second chance with Taylor.

For a few minutes, we skate in silence, hands clasped as Bruno Mars croons about loving his woman, just the way she is. Exactly how I feel about Taylor.

"How's this for our song?" I ask her, risking my balance for a glance at her.

She grins. "I like it. Not sure how much it fits us though."

"I think it might." I squeeze her hand. "Maybe more than you know."

Even under the lights, which have dimmed for this song, I can see the blush that deepens her cheeks.

"You think I'm beautiful?" she asks, looking surprised.

Her vulnerability kills me. Have her past boyfriends not told her enough? Does she really not know how gorgeous she is?

I'm about to tell her exactly how beautiful she is and how long I've wanted to tell her, when my wheels grind to a screeching halt. My body flies forward. And because I'm holding her hand and don't have the good sense to let go, I yank Taylor right along with me.

Her squeal alerts me to the fact that I'm about to knock her face-first into the rink. And like some kind of superhero in slow motion, I manage to twist my body, going down on my back to break her fall.

Only, a superhero wouldn't have felt the pain of his head cracking on the wood floor. For a moment, I'm seeing stars.

Nope, that's just the lights from the disco balls.

Taylor giggles, and my full attention snaps to her. She sort of crawls up my body to peer into my face, and suddenly this dirty wood floor is the best spot in the world. I could stay here all day.

"Hi," I say.

"Greetings," she says with a grin. "Are you okay there, champ?"

"Of course. Are you? Sorry for making you a casualty of war."

Taylor giggles again, and my eyes are drawn back to her mouth as she bites her lip before saying, "I'm not."

My eyes are drawn to her full pink lips. So very kissable. And so close to mine. Wait--is she getting closer?

I'm definitely not imagining it. She's moving closer. I sneak a glance at her eyes, and they're fixed on my mouth. This is good. This is *so* good.

It's the moment I've been hoping for, and a few dates early. I wouldn't have even tried for a kiss until at least holidate ten or eleven. But I'll take it!

I don't even care that it smells like old socks and that people are still whizzing by us like it's an everyday occurrence for two people to make out lying on the rink. Maybe it is.

Taylor's eyes flutter closed, and I'm just about to lift my head, closing off the final inches between us, when a little boy skates right over my hand.

And so instead of ending the date with a kiss, we end it in the ER, getting a splint on my two broken fingers.

DATES 6, 7, & 8

Taylor

"Are you sure you're up for this?" I ask after pulling out of the hospital parking lot. "Maybe we should just cut our losses and forget this holiday thing. I think it's cursed."

I glance over at Weston. It's strange to see him in the passenger seat of his car. But I insisted on driving. Partly because I don't want him driving one-handed and partly because the pain pills seem to be affecting him a little more than they should.

He glares at me. "No. Skating was no bueno. But I have hot cocoa at home and movies on the whatever it's called—"

"DVR?"

"The Netflix! Movies on the Netflix!"

I laugh. High on pain pills Weston is even more adorable than regular Weston.

"What was the third thing … I had one more thing … Date eight. Hey! That rhymes. Date eight!"

"Where's the list? I can look and figure it out."

"No!" Weston shouts. When my eyebrows shoot up, he softens his voice to a theatrical whisper. "I mean, no *thank you*. You can't see it. It's my own. My preciousss."

I laugh. "You're such a dork."

"I'm *your* dork," he says, and I wish that were true, and not just the pills talking.

Though … that moment in the skating rink. I didn't imagine that, did I? I swear I almost kissed him, right there on the rink floor. Or maybe he just hit his head hard and I mistook his dazed expression for something else. Hard to say since the moment got cut short by his broken fingers.

We're almost at his apartment, and I'm betting he'll fall asleep five minutes into the first movie, whatever it is. He hasn't told me, because after the infamous Night of Chad, Weston has kept the list hidden from me. I have to say that watching movies with hot cocoa sounds like a massive improvement after roller skating, which was fun. Until it wasn't.

I should at least stay until he sleeps, but that leaves me wondering how I'll get home. I could borrow his car, but that will be an issue in the morning with work. Maybe a ride share? I'm not a huge fan of taking those alone at night, but I'm definitely not calling my mom to ask for a ride home from Weston's. She'll get the wrong idea and start naming her grandbabies, if she hasn't already. Our moms have dreamed of us getting married for as long as we've known each other. I always rolled my eyes, pretending that deep down, I didn't wish for the same thing.

A soft snore comes from the passenger seat. Weston has conked out, his mouth slightly open. How can he be attractive even when he's drooling? It's simply unfair how genetically blessed the man is.

The splint on his hand makes me cringe every time I look at it. The doctor in the ER said the pain would subside soon. Weston should be back to full use of his left hand within two to six weeks. Not a huge deal. Although I doubt filling out spreadsheets one-handed is going to be fun at work.

The sight of the splint is a visible reminder of how I almost kissed Weston right in the middle of a roller rink.

Maybe I need a visual reminder, a sort of caution flag to steer me away, because more and more lately, I find myself drawn to Weston. I've tamped down my feelings for years. I dated other guys, guys that I even liked, though if I'm honest with myself, not one of them ever compared to Weston.

If I'm REALLY honest with myself, I know that I'm in love with my best friend.

And I could have kept it hidden if not for these holidays. Now I feel like he's going to see it in every look, hear it in every word. It was so sweet of him to want to get me through my breakup with Chad. Honestly, it worked. I haven't thought about Chad in days, other than to use his name as a new curse word, which is surprisingly satisfying.

I can't believe I gave the guy so much of my time. I planned my life around him, thinking we'd get married. And now? Nothing. Because the reality is that the only guy I've ever really wanted is the one snoring and drooling into his beard.

"We're here, big guy," I say once I've parked.

He snorts, blinking and looking around wildly for a moment before he smiles.

"I live here," he says.

"Yes. You do. Now let's see if we can get you up the stairs without breaking any more bones, okay?"

Weston holds his hand out in front of him, examining the splint. "Cool. I've never broken a bone."

"Well, now you've doubled up. Congrats, overachiever."

When we reach the top of the stairs, Weston pats his pockets, and I jangle the keys in front of him. "I've got it."

He hugs me from the side, his hot breath on my neck making my whole body shudder. "You're the best."

"I know. You are too. Let's get you inside."

He keeps hanging on me, making our entry into the apartment a little awkward. Honestly, I relish in the feel of his weight on my body, the scent of him, and the easy affection.

If only it were this easy ALL the time.

As soon as we're through the door, he lets me go, snatching a paper off the kitchen counter. It's the list! I'm dying to see it now that he's being so secretive, but even in his current state, he holds it so I can't read it.

"I've got it! Date eight!"

His eyes light up, and he folds the paper before clamping it between his teeth. And then he starts shedding his clothes.

"Uh, West," I say with a nervous laugh as he drops his long sleeve shirt on top of his jacket. Next up is the T-shirt he wore underneath, and when he peels that off, all forms of speech elude me.

Because sometime in the last few years, Weston has become a MAN. Not that I hadn't noticed the way he filled out during our college years, his broad shoulders balancing out his tall frame in a way they hadn't before. But I haven't seen him shirtless since we were in high school.

My, what a difference a few years and clearly a lot of hours in the gym make.

Weston is *ripped*. Like, give the man a puppy and he could be the model for one of those yearly calendars. There are more than enough muscles for each of the twelve months. We're talking weekly or daily calendar level.

I didn't even think of myself as the kind of girl who cared about a hot bod. Maybe on someone other than Weston, I wouldn't. But it *is* Weston, and my poor little heart doesn't stand a chance around all those pectorals and abdominals and other -als whose names I don't know. He's even got those deep lines leading down to his hip bones.

Which I'm noticing now because *he's taking off his pants*.

I slap a hand over my eyes, mostly not peeking through my fingers. "West! What are you doing?!"

"Date number eight, baby!"

At least, I think that's what he says, since he's talking around the paper still clenched between his teeth.

I hear the sound of his belt hitting the floor and I spin with a squeal, giving him my back. Because I don't know how far he's taking this, or what exactly this date eight entails, but I'm definitely not ready for this.

"Date number eight involves nudity?!"

"No, silly. Be right back!"

I hear the sound of him jogging away. Hopefully, he won't hurt himself.

I turn back around, biting my lip at the sight of his discarded clothes on the floor. I walk them to the stacked washer and dryer in the kitchen pantry, noticing that West has set out everything we need for hot cocoa. He's even bought different flavors: dark chocolate, mint, and raspberry. I start simmering the milk on the stove, swallowing around the lump in my throat. In all the years we dated Chad never did anything this thoughtful for me. No grand gestures; no small ones either. Meanwhile, Weston has gone out of his way to plan all of these special things.

And he isn't even my boyfriend. For a moment I'm overcome with a hot flare of jealousy thinking about how he must have treated his girlfriends if this is how he treats me, his *friend*.

Weston emerges from his bedroom with a huge smile on his face and …

"Christmas pajamas?"

I'm relieved and disappointed by the fact that his chest is no longer on display. I don't know if I could make it through a movie with him shirtless, though I certainly would have loved to try. But he looks adorable in a red and green flannel pajama set.

He counts on his good fingers. "Date numbers six, seven, and eight: watch Christmas movies while drinking hot cocoa in matching Christmas pajamas. Here."

Weston holds out a set of folded pajamas balanced on his palm. They're exactly the same as his, only in my size. When I just stare, he shakes them at me.

"Come on. Date number eight. Go put them on. I'll set up the movies but you should probably handle the cocoa."

"I already started it," I say, my voice sounding shaky and unsure. I'm thankful that Weston is under the influence of pain pills because if he were aware, he would definitely notice the tears I'm trying to hold back. This is all just too much. Weston is too much. I want for this so badly to be more than just a week of our lives, a handful of dates to help me get over Chad. I want this to be real.

Locking myself in West's bathroom, I clutch the pajamas to my chest and try to shove down the swell of emotion.

I love Weston.

And these dates are killing me. Because I know that at the end, we'll just go back to being friends who hang out every so often, when we're not too busy or not dating other people.

THE TWELVE HOLIDATES

I groan, again hating the thought of him dating other people.

I can't do this anymore. I can't *just* be his friend. But I've already put myself out there and he rejected me.

He was just a dumb kid. Things have changed. Don't be such a scaredy cat! Just tell him how you feel. Or better yet, show *him.*

I stare at myself in his mirror, trying to work up the courage. Making a confession isn't the best idea when he's basically high. Or maybe it's the best idea, because he won't have his guard up. He'll be more honest.

And maybe he won't remember. So if I tell him how I feel, or try to ask him how he feels, tomorrow he may not even know. It won't mess things up.

Resolved, I slip into the pajamas, which, of course, fit perfectly. Because Weston seems to have planned this down to the tiniest detail. That's how he is, how he's always been. Just one of the many things I love about him.

Is it possible that he could love me too? That he could be hiding the same secret I am? He has been different this week. More attentive. More flirtatious. More physical.

But I shake off the thought. Too many years have passed. Surely, he would have told me at some point.

When I get back to the kitchen, I've scalded the milk, and it takes a few minutes to wash the pan and start again. Weston is spread out on the couch when I get there, and he pats the spot right next to him. I set the cocoa on the table and settle in, warmed by the way he throws his arm around me and tucks me into his side.

"Ready?"

No. But I nod, because he's talking about the movie, not my decision to try and suss out his feelings for me.

Weston presses play, squeezing his arm around me tighter

when I groan. "*Die Hard*? Really? We've been over this. *Not* a Christmas movie."

"Shh. Don't ruin it for me. Every time I watch it, I pretend like it's the first time. You can always focus on Bruce Willis in his prime, when he still had hair."

"I do like hairy Bruce Willis."

Weston chuckles and I sigh, allowing myself to relax, pressing my cheek into the soft flannel of his shirt, all too aware now of the hard muscles underneath.

Moments later, I drift to sleep.

I'M AWARE OF MOVEMENT, the sensation of being lifted and carried. Groaning, I start to stir.

"Shh," Weston's familiar voice says, close to my ear. "I've got you."

His voice, his scent, his strong arms are so comforting that I allow myself to sink into him. I don't want to open my eyes, to let myself fully wake up. I don't want this moment, dream or reality, to end.

Weston settles me into his bed, tucking the covers up around me, before starting to turn away. I hate the loss of his touch. Fumbling to free my hand from the sheets, I grab his sleeve, opening my eyes just enough to see his handsome face in the dimly lit room.

"Stay," I whisper. It's half command, half plea.

I'm immediately embarrassed, feeling so vulnerable that I jerk my hand back under the covers. I can read the indecision on his face, though the expression in his eyes is not one I've seen before.

Finally, he gives me a slight nod, then with a tilted grin, he roughly climbs over me, making sure to jostle and squish me into the mattress as much as possible. I giggle, though it's all I can do not to grab him and pull him closer.

He settles next to me, close enough that I'm aware of him, but not so close that we're touching.

I'm facing away from him, listening to his breathing, fully awake now. I feel like every nerve ending has been summoned for duty, all standing at attention, ready to be called into action.

If I just turn, we'll be face to face. It would be so easy to be brave in the darkness, with the thin veil of sleep softening everything. But I cannot make myself move. Even here, in the dark and the wee hours of the morning, I'm too frightened of the cost. Of what I might lose if Weston doesn't want me.

"West?" I whisper.

"Yeah?"

Why didn't you kiss me back? Why didn't you want me?

If I kissed you now, would you respond differently?

The words are glued inside me. Stuck. They feel too huge, and yet so simple, as simple as words scrawled on a piece of notebook paper: *Do you like me? Check yes or no.*

"Goodnight," I say, because I just can't take the leap.

There's a shuffling in the bed and I feel a gentle press to my hair—a kiss. It's so sweet that tears prick my eyes.

"Sweet dreams, sugar plum," West says.

And so I lie in Weston's bed, feeling so close and yet so far from what I want most in the world, listening as his breath deepens into sleep.

DEAR DR. LOVE

From: Taylor556@DrLove.advice
To: DrLove@DrLove.advice

Dear Dr. Love

I know you get these kinds of letters all the time, but I'm in love with my best friend. He's everything to me, which is why I can't tell him how I feel.

But I can't sit by and NOT tell him either.

Years of friendship are at risk if I tell him and he doesn't feel the same way. My heart is at risk whether I tell him or not.

Is there some way to gauge how he feels? I finally think I'm ready to take the leap, but I'd really like a safety net.

Sincerely,
Fearful of Falling

———

From: DrLove@DrLove.advice

DEAR DR. LOVE

To: Taylor556@DrLove.advice

Dear Fearful,

You're right! If I had a dollar for every message I get about secretly being in love with a friend, I'd be off living on an island somewhere, sipping a margarita.

One reason this is so common is that lasting love can grow out of friendship. In fact, the best romantic relationships, the ones that really last, are between people who have a deep friendship, whether it came first or builds over time.

You want a safety net? Ask yourself some questions. They might reveal how your friend is feeling.

Does he treat you differently? Does he do special things for you? Does he remember your drink order, your birthday, your daily habits?

Does he check out other women when you're around? Does he seem jealous if other guys pay attention to you?

Sometimes people hide their feelings really well. But usually they leak out, in one way or another.

Look for the signs. Then ask yourself if it's worth the risk to your friendship to tell him, or if it's too risky NOT to.

-Dr. Love

PS- Taylor, you want to talk??

DATES 9 & 10

Taylor

SAM LEANS a hip against the edge of my desk. "Do you want to talk about the email you sent me?"

I expected this when I wrote Dr. Love an email from my personal account. I guess that means I want to talk about it, since I didn't create a fake email through the website. I could have just started a conversation, but somehow it was easier to type it out. Thankfully, she didn't start with "I told you so."

I put my hands over my face. "I just don't know what to do. But I can't keep living like this."

"All the time you and Weston are spending together is bringing the feelings out, huh?"

I nod, sinking back in my chair and looking up at Sam's deep brown eyes. My mind traces back over the past few days and all the hours I've spent with Weston. We see each other almost weekly, but the last time we spent this much time together was in high school.

I've *missed* him. Missed being around him so much—the laughter, the ease of conversation, and yeah, seeing him shirtless last night wasn't so bad either. Waking up in a cold bed with only a note from Weston … not so much.

Last night was torture. A big fat tease of a life I could imagine. One I want so badly that my heart feels like a clenched fist in my chest.

I woke up sometime when it was still dark to find our legs tangled together and his chest pressed against my back. I tried to stay awake just so I could savor every second, but I must have fallen back asleep. He had already gone to work by the time I woke, and it was the second most disappointing moment of my life.

Being the thoughtful guy he was, Weston left coffee, money for a rideshare, and a quick note that said he was looking forward to tonight, holidates nine and ten. I'm not even sure I can handle being around him again.

I sigh, looking down at my hands as I speak. "It's like those optical illusion paintings. The ones where you have to cross your eyes and unfocus until the hidden image becomes clear. I feel like I'm staring too hard to see this clearly."

Sam gives me a small smile. "That's a great analogy. What I hear you saying is that you need a little outside perspective."

"That's exactly what I need. I'm too close to the situation. Too close to *him*. Tell me what to do, Sam. Dr. Love. Whatever."

Sam sighs, absentmindedly working her dark hair into a braid. "From everything you've told me, Weston seems interested. Guy friends don't plan elaborate dates, not even to help you get over an ex."

Weston has been incredibly into this holidays thing. Despite the toxic s'mores, the awkward photo with Santa, and Weston's broken fingers, these have been some of the best dates of my life.

No. Not *some* of. THE best dates of my life. Because they were with Weston.

"Let me ask you this—has he shown any possessiveness?" Sam asks. "Like, did he get jealous or upset when you're dating other guys?"

My heart trips over itself and falls down a steep flight of stairs.

"No." I can tell by Sam's face this is bad, even though I already know. "I mean, he never really liked any of them. But the guys I dated ..."

I shrug, thinking of Chad. And Alann, whose choice to add an extra N to his name should have been a warning. Before him, it was a short list of guys who never should have made anyone's short list.

"They weren't exactly winners," Sam says.

"That's kind of an understatement. But no, Weston never really got possessive or jealous. That's a bad sign, isn't it?"

I don't really need her to answer. I can feel the truth of it. I couldn't stand to look any of Weston's girlfriends in the eye. I avoided meeting them whenever possible. Always. While he was just lukewarm about my exes.

Plus, I can't ignore the fact that last night we slept in the same bed. Emphasis on the word *slept*. Not that I would have wanted Weston to make ALL the moves. But he didn't make a *single* move. Not. A. One.

Doesn't that say it all?

Sam looks helplessly at me. But before she can say anything, not that anything she could say would help me feel better, my phone starts ringing. It's "The Imperial March," my mother's ringtone.

"Better get this," I say, waving my phone. "It's the mothership."

"I'm sorry, Taylor." Sam gives me a pat on the shoulder before heading back to her desk, slipping in earbuds.

I draw in a breath and answer. "Hey, Mom."

"Oh, Taylor! The Christmas Eve party is ruined! You won't believe it!"

Oh, yes. I will. Because my mom is the queen of drama. But my chest does feel tight at the mention of the Christmas Eve party, a tradition between Weston's family and mine. I don't know how I'm going to be around him and around our families without them guessing that something is up.

"What?"

"Please, just tell me you're still bringing Chad," Mom says.

I massage my forehead with my free hand, wishing I could smooth away this conversation like the furrow in my brow.

"About that."

Mom groans. "I just had this feeling! Oh, Taylor. Martha has really done it this time."

"What did she do?"

Usually my mom and Weston's mom get along like gangbusters, fueled mostly by their shared desire to see Weston and me walk down the aisle. I'm not sure what this has to do with Chad.

"She invited not one, but SEVERAL single women to the party for Weston. She's been flashing his picture around town like she's his pimp."

"That's a bit harsh, don't you think?"

"Maybe pimp is the wrong word, but it's just low. And if you don't have Chad ..."

It means I'll be dateless while Weston has a bevy of women. For once, I agree with Mom. This *will* ruin the Christmas party, one I always look forward to.

After my realization that Weston's lack of jealousy means he's not into me, I don't know that I can stomach watching other women throwing themselves at him. No way am I going to be a spectator in the Christmas Hunger Games with West as the prize. Nope. I think I feel the flu coming on.

"Does, uh, Weston know? About the women?"

He and I haven't talked at all about the party. I just assumed we'd ride together, something we do on years we don't bring dates. I squeeze my eyes closed.

"Weston encouraged her to ask them. According to Martha, he told her to ask her barista. One of them is a *model*. Can you believe it?"

I don't want to believe it. But my ribs are folding in on themselves, collapsing over the hollow space in my chest where my heart used to be.

"What happened with Chad? We can't have you coming single. Not with all these interlopers."

If we were talking about anything else, I'd laugh at her use of the word interlopers. But nothing about this is funny.

"I'm not coming."

"You have to come! This is family! Absolutely not!"

"Mom," I groan. "I can't. I just can't."

She's uncharacteristically quiet for a beat or two. Then she says quietly, "You finally figured out that you have feelings for him, didn't you?"

"Yeah, Mom. I did. And he doesn't feel the same way."

"Oh, Taylor. Are you sure?"

No. Yes. No. Yes.

"Pretty positive."

She harrumphs. "That sounds like a twenty-percent positive. I can work with that. What we need to do is find you a date to make him jealous."

Except Weston wouldn't be jealous. That's exactly the thing. "Mom. A date is the last thing I need. Seriously. No."

"Don't think of it like a date. It has to be someone really great though. Not like the other guys you've brought home."

"Did no one like *any* of my boyfriends?"

"I'm not going to dignify that with a response. Now, I've got a few ideas. But if you find someone first, tell me. Because we aren't turning you into the Bachelorette. I have some self-respect, unlike Martha."

"Clearly."

When I'm done with my conversation, I turn to Sam. She pulls out her earbuds.

"So, you need a date?" she asks.

"I thought you were listening to music," I accuse.

"I was listening to music. And your conversation. I can help, you know. I've got just the guy for the job. It will be totally platonic, but trust me--if someone was going to make Weston jealous, this is the guy."

I sigh, my breath thin and raspy. "Okay."

Sam grins wickedly, a look I don't like at all. "You won't regret this."

The problem is, I already do.

―――

"Are you sure nothing's wrong?" Weston asks, maybe for the fifth time.

What a loaded question. I'm quite sure that *everything* is wrong. Not the least of which is the foundation of our gingerbread house, which has a distinct lean. The structural soundness is something I can fix, so I focus on that. Not the weird awkwardness between me and Weston.

"Piping bag," I say, holding out my hand.

Weston holds out the bag, then yanks it back. His fierce eyes pin me in place. "Tell me," he demands. "Is it me? Did I do something? Is it *Chad*?"

He grimaces as he says Chad's name. But it's not jealousy, I remind myself. It's just plain old dislike. Because Weston doesn't feel the same way I do.

"Is someone *being* a Chad?" Weston is trying another tactic, joking with me since serious and scary isn't working.

I roll my eyes and grab the bag of icing. *"You're* being a Chad."

"Our gingerbread house is being a Chad. How long until they disqualify us, do you think?"

For date nine, Weston entered us in a gingerbread house challenge put on by a local culinary school. Which means that our basic rectangular house is competing against the Frank Lloyd Wrights of gingerbread architecture.

I'm not even sure how he got us into this event, which definitely looks like the kind to have had an entrance fee. More than one judge in a white chef's coat has stopped by our work station, stared in disbelief at our crooked attempt, then glared at us before moving on. I wish we could blame Weston's broken fingers, but this sad attempt is all on me.

I straighten up the back wall, not ready to give up yet. At least, not on this. We won't win, not even close, but our house will not collapse on my watch. I pipe out another thin layer of icing, then prop the wall up at a ninety-degree angle.

"Gumdrop," I say, holding out my hand like I'm a surgeon, asking for a scalpel.

Weston drops a red one in my palm. There's a bite missing.

"West," I groan. "Why did you even enter us in this if you were going to sabotage our efforts?"

He gives me an unrepentant grin and pops the whole gumdrop in his mouth. I grab another one from the pile.

Weston waits so long to answer that I almost forget I've asked a question. "It's for charity," he says.

Nudging my shoulder and directing my attention toward a sign that bears the name of the one nonprofit I support year after year, a home for women and their children who have escaped domestic abuse.

The tip of my piping bag stops in the line of shingles I was drawing on the roof. It trembles in my hand.

"This is actually dates nine *and* ten," West says. "Nine—build a gingerbread house. And ten—give to someone less fortunate."

"That wasn't on the list," I say, trying to force back the tears in my eyes by the sheer force of my will.

"I added it," he says. "The dates were all a little self-centered anyway. Giving felt right."

"That's really nice," I say. "How much was it to enter? I can contribute too." I sniff.

"Don't worry about it," he says, trying to put an arm around my shoulders. I pull away and set the piping bag down, before pulling out my phone.

Less than a minute later, I've got the website pulled up for this event. Five hundred dollars. That's how much Weston paid to enter us in the competition. That's how much will go to the nonprofit, because all the other expenses like the materials, the space, and the judges' time were donated.

Why does he have to be so perfect? So nice, so fun, so thoughtful?

"I don't know what to say."

Weston reaches for my hand. It feels so good to be touched by him. I should pull away, but I can't.

"Say you'll go with me tomorrow night to the Christmas Eve party," he says.

My head swings to his as he keeps talking. He squeezes my hand, and it's like a direct line to my heart.

"Come with me as my date."

Did I just say he was thoughtful? Nice? Nah. Forget that. The man is a terrorist dictator of some small country. I yank my hand away.

I hold his gaze, hoping he can see the fury. "I thought you *had* a date. Or was it two? Something about a barista and a model. What's one more for good measure?"

I want to see surprise on his face. Confusion. Because a part of me hoped that he didn't know about the dates his mom set up. I wanted Mom to be wrong. Instead of confusion, Weston blinks at me steadily, looking wary and resigned.

"Don't worry about them. My mom set it up. I don't know any of them."

"So, there *are* other women coming to be your date? And you still thought you'd ask me. As what--your backup?"

"It's not like that."

"It seems that way to me."

His eyes flash with anger, or maybe determination. "Taylor--"

The big clock in front of all the work stations finally reaches zero and an alarm goes off. Time is up. I stand, not even bothering to take off my apron. We lost. What does it matter?

"I already have a date," I tell him, grabbing my bag as I head for the door. All I can think about is getting out, getting air, getting some distance between Weston and me.

"Taylor, wait!"

Weston reaches me when I'm almost to my car, his long legs eating up the distance between us. I'm so thankful that this place was close to my work. I wouldn't have been able to handle a ride home with him right now.

"Taylor!"

I pause, facing my driver's side door. I can see his reflection in the window in front of me, distorted in the curved glass. He runs his good hand through his hair, then shoves it in the pocket of his jeans. He must have left his coat inside.

"How do you have a date for the Christmas Eve party?"

Because Sam, feeling sorry for me, set me up with a friend of a friend.

"The usual way dates happen, Weston."

"You asked someone?"

He's so still behind me, eyes boring into my back. I can see the tightness of his jaw, the rigid line of his shoulders.

Is this jealousy?

I'm too emotional right now to have a reaction. Coming to grips with my feelings this week has been too much effort. Holding so much back, questioning every move he makes. I'm exhausted.

"I did. Because you already have multiple dates. I didn't want to be alone."

"You wouldn't have been alone. I wanted to go with you. I thought after this week we've had …" Weston starts to speak, then trails off, shaking his head and turning to stare into the hills rising up above the parking lot.

"What did you think?" I ask, carefully.

Just tell me how you feel. One way or the other. Put me out of my misery.

Though, I guess if he rejects me, I'd be in more misery.

But a few words of assurance from him would burn off this fog of emotion instantly. I bite my lip, not wanting to hope.

I see the moment he shifts, shoulders sagging, chin dipped low to his chest. There was a time I could read West so easily, when I knew what he was feeling, and usually why. This is defeat, but it's a reaction I don't understand.

I debate spinning around, grabbing him by his stupid shirt and yanking his lips to mine in a kiss. No way to misinterpret that. No way to come back from it either. Not a second time.

"I'll see you tomorrow night," Weston says, finally.

If that's not a period at the end of the sentence, I don't know what is.

DATES 11, 12, & LUCKY 13

Weston

I CAN'T BELIEVE SO MUCH of my success tonight rests in the hands of my two younger brothers. I swing my gaze between the two big idiots, doing my best to look like I'll totally annihilate them if they mess this up.

But who am I kidding? Seth and Aaron have never been intimidated by me. I may have finally filled out in a way that's proportional to my height, but my brothers play defense for Texas A & M. They're monsters. Standing shoulder to shoulder as they are right now, they could take out a water buffalo.

"We've got this, big bro," Seth says, clapping a meaty hand on my back.

"We'll follow the pretty ladies and keep them away from you. Easy. They won't be looking at you when they see us anyway," Aaron says, puffing out his chest. Probably true.

I roll my eyes. "Nice and humble. Just what the ladies love."

"Oh, trust me. We know what ladies love," Seth says.

Forget what I said about taking out water buffalo. My brothers *are* the buffalo. Or maybe more like wild hogs. Either way, they're definitely animals.

They break like this was a football huddle and start moving away, probably to the kitchen to get their egg nog on.

"By the way, I never said they were pretty!" I call. "Mom picked them, so who knows. Either way, you agreed!"

They rumble something from the kitchen that I hope is an agreement. That will have to do. If I had done a better job this week with Taylor, I wouldn't need their help. If only I had just laid it all on the line rather than trying to slowly woo her with dates that ended up being more ridiculous than romantic...

But she just went through a big breakup, I remind myself. Easing into this seemed like a wise decision.

A *safe* decision. It was too safe. And after years of loving Taylor, I should have played it anything but safe. Now, no thanks to Mom, Taylor thinks I'm dating half of Austin.

Tonight is going to be a train wreck. I know it. This *should* have been our last two holidays, plus a bonus one I added. Lucky number thirteen.

Instead Taylor will be with some other guy. I already want to punch him in the face, whoever he is.

I do understand why she was upset about the women Mom enlisted to come. I should have mentioned it to Taylor, so she knew I wasn't in on it. I knew, but I didn't agree. And I really didn't think Mom would invite *more* women. I should have insisted Mom uninvite them. But I didn't. I can't blame Taylor for coming with a date when she thought I had *multiple* dates.

And yet ... it stings. I really thought we were building toward something this week, that we had taken steps forward. I know I didn't imagine the attraction blooming between us. The night we spent together in my bed, it felt like we were both struggling with restraint. Maybe I should have given in and let myself kiss her the way I wanted to.

I've wanted to do things right. And stealing a first kiss without telling her how I feel and while impacted by pain meds definitely didn't feel right. Tempting, but not right.

Now I'm trusting that my two muscle-headed brothers will play their best defense ever against the women Mom invited tonight. Hopefully there are only the two I know of: Gisele, the foot model (not to be confused with Gisele the supermodel), and a barista named Kitten. Yes. Her name is Kitten.

"Who agreed to what?"

Grandma's voice startles me, and I turn to see her coming out from behind the dining room curtains. Was she hiding behind there? I shouldn't be surprised. Though she's rail thin and slightly stooped, her bright eyes have the same glittering and deadly quality as a vampire from a horror movie.

"Uh, Grandma. Hi. I didn't see you there."

Hiding behind the curtains like a psychopath.

"That's the point, boy."

She laughs, and it makes the hairs stand up on my arms. It is the definition of a cackle. We should invite her to pass out our Halloween candy every October. It would be like having our own little haunted house.

"Now, boy. What are you plotting?"

I blink at her, watching as she lifts a coffee mug to her lips. Three guesses as to what's inside, and not one of those guesses is non-alcoholic.

"It's nothing." I wave a hand dismissively, forcing out a laugh.

Her beady little eyes narrow, and she throws back whatever is in her mug before slamming it on the table. Wiping her mouth with the back of her wrinkled hand, she steps closer. I fight the urge to tuck tail and run.

I know she's my Grandma, my dad's mom. My blood. But she's at best, intimidating, and at worst, terrifying.

"What is it? A prank? Kidnapping? A bit of light treason? I want in. These parties are always boring."

The scent of alcohol and, inexplicably, something like cotton candy wafts from her to me. She must see me sniffing, because she says, "Whipped cream vodka. Best invention of the twenty-first century. Now, are you going to tell me what you're up to?"

A finger lands on my chest, and I swear, the thing is like a talon. I weigh my options. I could let my Grandma, who hates Taylor, know about my desperate last-ditch plan to confess my feelings. Or I can refuse to tell her and potentially have my soul stolen, dismantled, and sold for parts.

"Are you sure you want to help? It's … about *love*." I clear my throat, waiting as though for test results at the doctor's office when I'm pretty sure I already have strep throat.

"Love is—" She pauses, licking her dry lips as her eyes continue to glitter at me like they're lit from within.

My mind tries to fill in the blank. You just never know with Grandma.

Love is …

Stupid.

For sissies.

Vile.

"Love is the only thing worth doing in this life," she says.

I realize the glittering in her eyes is tears and not the

flickering of torches lit from the underworld. Grandma is ... emotional?

I barely remember my Grandpa, other than to know he was the gentlest, sweetest man on the planet. If Halloween is the holiday I associate with Grandma, Christmas would have been his. He was like a big, jolly old St. Nick. Maybe he softened her edges? I can't remember Grandma any way other than this.

Grandma sniffs, and I find myself pulling her into a hug. I can't remember the last time I wrapped my arms around her. She doesn't *do* affection.

"What is this?" She wiggles away from me, and one of her bony elbows almost punctures my spleen.

"A hug, Grandma."

"No hugging! Now, tell me of this love plot. After you get me more vodka."

I pick up her mug, unsure if I should be feeding the beast, so to speak. Before I can hit up the makeshift bar in the kitchen, Grandma raises her hand.

"Wait! Who's the lucky woman?"

Oh boy. "It's Taylor," I refuse to let my voice falter or my eyes drift away from hers. "It's always been Taylor."

Her nose lifts. "That little tart from down the street with the dark hair and killer bod?"

I choke out a laugh that sounds more like a smoker's cough. "That's the one."

Grandma's face tightens, and her eyes narrow. "I always did like that one."

I stare at her in disbelief. "The last time you came for Christmas Eve, you called her a communist."

Grandma shrugs. "Your point? I happen to like commies."

Okay, then. Time to get Grandma a refill.

I think overall, my chances of this working just went

down considerably, but then again, were they ever that high to begin with?

Taylor

IF I WASN'T ALREADY in love with Weston, however unrequited my love might be, I would be all about Chase.

When I open my apartment door to find him standing there, a crooked smile on his handsome face and a single red rose in hand, I urge my heart to beat faster, or at least to give a little flutter.

Instead, like a car engine that's dying, it heaves a groaning sigh and gives up.

"You must be Sam's friend, Taylor," he says. "I'm Chase."

I just stand there, somehow frozen into immobility, until he glances at the number beside my door. "Am I at the right place?"

"Sorry." I shake my head and manage a smile. "I'm Taylor. Good to meet you. I'm being awkward. I don't usually do the whole blind date thing. Or whatever this is."

"Me neither." Chase holds out the rose. "I know red roses are the romantic heavy hitters in the flower family, but because it's Christmas, it was this or a potted poinsettia."

I laugh, taking the flower from his hands. Our fingers brush and I have no reaction to the contact.

"This is great. Thanks. I won't read too much into it. Let me get it in some water."

"I'll wait out here," Chase says, shoving his hands in his pockets. "Stranger danger and all that."

I smile and leave him on the porch. Sam didn't give me much information about Chase, other than to say he wasn't looking for romance either and that I could trust him. It seemed perfect at the time. But the idea of showing up with someone other than Weston tonight has nausea rolling through my belly.

"Let's just say I think it will be win-win for both of you," she had said, her eyes twinkling. I didn't want to ask.

I study him as I follow him down to his car, a Jeep that looks like it actually might see some off-road action. Chase, too, looks like he spends time outdoors, or at least in a gym. He's closer to my height than Weston, with broad shoulders, dark brown hair, and a trim beard.

He smiles as he opens the door for me, and I can't help but notice the way his biceps strain against his polo shirt. Still doesn't compare to Weston shirtless.

"You won't be cold?" I ask him, nodding toward his short sleeves.

The temperature has warmed up overnight, fickle as Texas can be, but it's not *warm*. I'm still wearing long sleeves and a sweater.

"I'm always hot," he says. Then, shuffling, he glances down at his feet. "I mean, temperature wise."

"I know what you meant." I can't help but smile. I can see his blush even in the dark.

"Good. Wouldn't want you to think I'm some kind of egomaniac." He shuts my door and jogs around to the driver's side.

This guy is too cute. And so nice I feel a little bad that essentially he's here with me as my human shield or fake date. I take a deep breath as he gets in and starts the car.

"I probably need to prepare you for tonight. What did Sam tell you, exactly?"

Chase gives me a sideways glance, a small smile on his face. "Not much, just that she had a friend in need of a non-date date. Why don't you tell me about tonight?"

How much do I share? I consider for only a moment, then decide that I'll probably never see Chase again. Might as well go with brutal honesty.

"I'm in love with my best friend, and I'm pretty sure he doesn't love me back. This is a joint family Christmas party. Our mothers have always wanted to set us up … until this year. When apparently his Mom decided to invite a bunch of eligible women for him to meet tonight."

Chase grimaces. "Wow. Okay. So, do we need to pretend to date, or …?"

My cheeks feel hot at the underlying question, which seems to be, *How far are we going to take this thing?*

"No. I mean, honestly, I just need someone in my corner. We don't have to, um, do more than that. Just stick with me. If that's okay."

He draws in a quick breath. "I don't mind. Really. I can totally commiserate with your situation. That's probably why Sam suggested me."

I wait for him to say more, but he doesn't, and then we're pulling up to Weston's house. It looks all lit up from within, bringing back so many memories of so many years. It all hits me square in the chest, and I clutch the gift that I've brought for his parents.

"Anything else I need to know? Any other ways I can help?" Chase asks.

I don't deserve his kindness. Not when I'm basically using him. Though I guess if he knows about it up front, it isn't quite so bad. Chase seems willing, maybe because of whatever makes him able to relate.

I think about how much to tell him without making him

bolt. "Well, Weston's grandma will be here. She's pretty ruthless. And their dog may bite your ankles. He bites everyone. Just watch your pant legs."

Chase nods. So far, so good. But I'm not done.

"Don't be surprised if his brothers walk around with mistletoe on a fishing pole. They're linebackers for A&M so no one messes with them. The eggnog is *very* spiked, and sometimes the night ends with a game of backyard fruitcake dodgeball, which is vicious but ends quickly. Either by injury or the fruitcakes disintegrating."

I look at Chase, who only blinks at me. "You're not running away?" I ask.

Chase laughs. "Sounds like a party to me. You ready?"

"Nope." I grin. "So, let's go."

THE PARTY IS the same as every other year, except for the dull ache in my heart, Chase's comforting presence, and the two women draping themselves over Weston like cheap IKEA curtains.

It's hard to watch, even though Weston doesn't seem the slightest bit interested in either woman. I've never been so thankful for his brothers, who have been prying the women off him like they're barnacles. Eventually, it works, and the women shift their attention to Seth and Aaron, which lessens the jealousy moving through me like a menopausal heat map.

Meanwhile, our mothers seem locked in a silent death match, and our fathers keep going out back to smoke cigars and escape the tension.

All in all, worst Christmas Eve party ever.

Except for one saving grace, the only thing that has kept me from sprinting out the door. And that thing is the dark look that has haunted Weston's face whenever he's looked at me. Or, more specifically, at Chase and me.

Because if I had to name it, that expression on Weston's face would be jealousy. That or murderous rage, because it matches the expression Weston's grandma always wears. I've always wondered if they were actually related. Now, there is absolutely no question in my mind.

I've been avoiding Weston all night. Which is why I'm in the kitchen, pointedly bypassing the eggnog and wolfing down the cheese ball no one seems to like but me.

"Getting reinforcements?"

I shouldn't be surprised that Chase is the one who finds me. He hasn't left my side for most of the night. Whether because he's scared of Grandma or just trying to support me, it's been nice.

Still, Weston is usually the one who would track me down if I'm upset. The fact that he hasn't is disappointing now that I thinking about it.

"I'm eating my feelings," I tell Chase.

He looks down at my plate, then makes a face. "Is that a cheese ball?"

"I know. Disgusting, right?"

Chase leans over the counter, crossing his muscular forearms. "I mean, compared to fruitcake, it's not so bad. Or whatever that purple stuff was on the buffet."

I have a mouthful of crackers, so I throw a hand over my face, laughing. Before I manage to respond, a voice comes from the doorway.

"It's beet salad," Grandma says.

Chase and I both straighten up. I've managed not to be alone with her, just as I've managed to keep my pant legs away from Uncle Tony's snappy jaws.

"Hi, Grandma," I say. "The beet salad was wonderful, as always."

"You didn't eat it," she says. "Or your teeth would be purple. No matter. You look good. Your breasts look larger. They've grown from apples to cantaloupes. I see now why he loves you."

My eyes fly to Chase, whose face has turned a color closely resembling the beet salad I lied about eating.

"I, uh ..." Chase fumbles for words, his eyes going everywhere in the room except my (apparently cantaloupe-sized) breasts.

Grandma waves a hand. "Not you, muscle boy. I mean my grandson."

Weston ... *loves me?*

No. That can't be right, despite the way hope rockets through me like the cork of a champagne bottle. Everyone knows that we don't listen to Grandma.

But ... could she be right?

Not about my breasts, which haven't grown since eighth grade. I just wear the right size bra now, though it's helpful to know it's working.

ANYWAY.

Could she be right that Weston *does* have feelings for me? Jealousy was the only thing I hadn't seen in him, but tonight, he's got it in spades.

Chase gives me a hopeful smile, his eyebrows raised. I like the fact that it feels like he's on my team, hoping right along with me that Weston has feelings for me.

"Grandma, there you are." Weston strides into the room and steers his grandma toward the living room. "Mom was looking for you," he says. She mutters a few things under her breath but doesn't protest. I wonder how much Weston heard.

Once Grandma is gone, Weston spins back to face Chase and me, that same look on his face. Dark, angry, jealous. I don't know how exactly to describe it other than to say it's intense. Quite a contrast with the red Santa hat he's worn all night. But it works for him.

The fierceness on his face makes me want to attack him. (With my mouth, not my fists, in case that wasn't clear.) Instead, I grip the edge of the counter so hard my fingers ache.

"We need to talk," Weston says, his eyes burning right through me. Then his gaze swings to Chase. "Without *him*."

Chase crosses his arms. Whatever he's missing in height compared to Weston, he makes up for in bulk. He looks at me, searching my face.

"Are you okay?" Chase asks.

I still feel no romantic inclinations toward the man, but he's going to make some woman *very* happy.

"I'm ... okay."

"I'll be right in there," Chase says to me. "In case you need me."

"You might need *me*," I tell him, smiling. "Grandma's in there. And Uncle Tony. Watch your pants."

Before leaving the room, Chase faces off with Weston. "As I said, I'll be right in there." The way he says it now is definitely a threat.

I swear, the two almost come to blows. To be completely, shamefully honest, part of me wouldn't mind seeing that. Not at all. Even with two fingers in a splint, my money is on Weston.

I probably need to go outside and have a very strong talk with myself.

Chase pushes by Weston and disappears into the family

room. And ... I'm alone with this moody, growly, unhinged version of my best friend. I hardly recognize him.

The silence between us is awkward. I wait for Weston to speak. He called this meeting, after all. Whatever happens next, whichever direction it goes, I won't be the one to put myself out there and say the first word. It *has* to be him.

So, I wait.

Finally, Weston speaks. "Every year, I make sure that cheese ball is here for you."

The ... *cheese ball*? I try to follow this train of thought, wondering if Weston hit the eggnog. I thought he wanted to talk about something important. Maybe to discuss Chase or the women his mother invited tonight or even the last few days of near-perfect dates.

Weston wants to talk about the *party snacks*?

"You—what?"

I'm suddenly furious. I've never been angry with Weston before this week. Not really. Only hurt. After so many years of repressing my feelings and then the last few days of actually realizing them, the anger is as refreshing as an after-dinner mint.

Weston moves closer until he's standing centimeters away. I glare up at him, my back pressed up against the counter's edge.

"The cheese ball," he says. "You're the only one who likes it."

If the anger is refreshing, his proximity is stifling. He's a fire, sucking up all the oxygen in the room. I place my palms lightly on his chest and shove.

Of course, he doesn't budge. And now I don't want to remove my hands. I remember what his chest looked like underneath the shirt, and my hands, which couldn't care less about the cheese ball or my anger, want to go exploring. I shake off that thought and narrow my eyes.

"After this week, after tonight, you want to talk about the *food*?"

I swear, Weston is expanding, getting larger, growing closer to me even as he just stands there. Without taking a step, it's like he's crowding right up against my heart.

"Every year, I buy the cheese ball and bring it. For *you*."

I throw my hands up. "Fine. You hate the cheese ball. Congratulations. Next year, I'll bring it. I get it."

I don't, not really, but I feel like he's telling me that he's tired of going out of his way for me. The anger steps aside, just enough hurt has room to surface. I fight the prick of tears at the backs of my eyes. I should go, before he reads on my face every feeling I've ever had for him. But Weston snaps his arms out, trapping me against the counter. It would be totally hot if I weren't already on the verge of an emotional breakdown.

"No," Weston says, "you *don't* get it."

And then, his mouth slants over mine so fast that I don't even have time to shout, Bingo, Yahtzee, or Hallelujah!

Weston's lips are on mine, his chest pressing close, his arms caging my body in place. Even if I could, I wouldn't move. Because our lips pressing together, his hot, sweet mouth opening against my own, THIS is the culmination of all my dreams.

Weston is kissing me!

This is no junior high kiss. The one I gave him back then was hardly more than a whisper. More of a platonic press of my dry lips to his. No movement. No passion. Just a whole lot of longing and inexperience. It was a plain white cracker, unsalted.

This? It's like a buffet of exotic foods exploding in my

mouth, rich and heady and delicious. It's a Godiva chocolate fountain. It's expensive champagne, the bubbles going straight to my head.

The kiss. Is. Everything.

I'm barely conscious, dragged under by the way Weston's lips caress mine. His good hand moves to my hip, gripping me possessively. The hand with the splint cups the back of my head as best he can. He tastes like peppermint and happily ever afters. He feels like my future, solid and secure.

Maybe there should be a weird transition from friendship to this, but this feels completely natural. Inevitable, really. It's like my body has simply been waiting for this moment, drumming its fingers along the arm of an uncomfortable chair, reading the boring waiting room magazines, until West threw open the door and called my name.

And now I'm the one who wants to be a barnacle, attaching myself to Weston. Except not even his beefy brothers could pry me off. Not now that I've finally got him. He's *mine*.

I pull back, and it takes all the willpower I have. Weston's eyes are hooded, fixed on my lips.

"Why were you going on about the cheese ball?" I ask. I *have* to know.

He groans softly. "Taylor. That's the first thing you say after that kiss?"

I can't help but look at his lips, which turn up into a grin. He's like a black hole, sucking me back in.

Apply brakes! Apply brakes!

I place my palm flat against his chest, keeping him at bay.

"You were the one who brought up the cheese ball. I'm just trying to figure out how we went to kissing after you complained about going out of your way to buy me a cheese ball."

"No. You misunderstood." Weston lifts his hands cupping my cheeks. "I wasn't being critical. I was trying to tell you that I love you."

I draw in a breath at his words. "You—wait. What?"

Weston's smile is slow, patient, like he's a man with all the time in the world. "I love you, Taylor. I have loved you for so long. That's what I was trying to tell you with the cheese ball."

Maybe I'm dense, but I don't get it.

"You were saying I love you with the *cheese ball?*"

Weston leans forward until his forehead rests on mine. "I swear to you, after tonight, I don't want to ever hear about the cheese ball again."

"Agreed."

"What I was trying to tell you, obviously badly, for years through the appetizer-who-shall-not-be-named and this week with all the holidates, is that I will do anything for you, Taylor."

"For years?"

"*Years.* Since before our first kiss. You surprised me with the kiss, which shocked me into awkward silence. Then you friendzoned me, and here we are today."

He pulls back and sweeps his fingertips over my cheeks, careful not to jab the splint in my eye. I want to tell Weston how much I love him. I hope he knows, that he can see it in my eyes, because my mouth won't form words.

I'm going back over the past in my mind. All the wasted time. All the other people we've dated who weren't each other. When all along, we were both right here.

"Stop it," Weston says, tapping my forehead with his splinted hand. "You're thinking too much."

"All the thoughts are about you. But if you want me to stop …" I shrug, grinning.

"I definitely don't mind your thoughts on me, and me alone. But I'd also like to hear that you love me."

"Pretty confident that I love you, huh?"

"Not confident. Just terribly hopeful and more than a little desperate."

"I love you, Weston. I think I have since we were thirteen."

I can feel a tension in his body release. He sags against me with a sigh, his soft lips meeting mine again, the scratch of his beard just what I need to ground me in this moment.

And that's when we hear it. The sound of a shout from the other room, glass breaking, and the unmistakable growling of Uncle Tony as he rips into an unlucky someone.

A female, accented voice squeals, "Not my feet! I need them for work!"

I can't help but laugh, dropping my head against Weston's chest. He's shaking with laughter too, and it only grows louder when we hear Grandma.

"If your feet are so important, you should have gotten them insured!"

When the chaos and our laughter dies down a little, Weston says, "Shall we end holidates eleven, twelve, and thirteen by making our moms the happiest they've ever been?"

"Absolutely! But wait—what were the dates tonight?"

"The holiday party was eleven. Grandma coming counts as visiting an old folks' home, as she brought the old folk to us. And as for number thirteen ..." Weston pulls off his Santa hat to reveal a leafy green bit of foliage tucked inside. "Kissing under the mistletoe."

I grin at him, then watch as he scratches the top of his head, then scratches some more. I glance down at the plant again.

"Um, West. Who gave you the mistletoe?"

"Aaron. Why?" He's still scratching, switching hands so he can use the splint.

"That's not mistletoe. It's a big ball of poison ivy."

His hand freezes in place on his head, and I see the moment it sinks in. "I'm going to kill him."

"With kindness?" I gingerly take the hat from him and dump the whole thing in the trash.

"No. With fruitcake. And my fists."

Weston leans in close, pressing a lingering kiss to my mouth. Then, he grabs a fruitcake off the counter and runs from the room, still scratching as he bellows his brother's name.

I lift my fingers to my lips, trying to memorize the feel of Weston's mouth on mine. Hopefully, I won't have to exist with only the memory of this one night of kissing. If I'm right about this, we'll have forever.

Assuming Weston doesn't end up in jail for assault with a deadly fruitcake first.

The Twelve Holidates

1. ~~Dress in something sexy and hide in a person-sized stocking in your significant other's bedroom~~ Burn the stocking in a ceremonial funeral pyre
2. Eat s'mores over a ~~campfire~~ burning stocking
3. Have a photo taken with Santa
4. Attend an ugly Christmas sweater event
5. Go ~~ice skating~~ roller skating
6. Watch Christmas movies
7. Drink homemade hot cocoa
8. Wear matching Christmas pajamas
9. Build a gingerbread house
10. Give to charity
11. Attend a holiday party
12. ~~Spread cheer at a nursing home~~ Try to survive the wrath of Grandma
13. Kiss the heck out of Taylor under the mistletoe

EPILOGUE

Taylor

"Why are we parked here, watching this random apartment building?"

I lean against the passenger door, crossing my arms and raising my eyebrows at Weston. He glances at his watch again.

"Patience, Iago," he says.

My fiancé—A term I'm going to use as much as possible until our wedding in six months—is the kind of man who still quotes random things like *Aladdin*. Saying yes to him? Best and easiest decision ever. I admire the ring on my finger before responding.

"I've been patient, but it's been like twenty minutes and you still won't tell me—"

"Shh! It's time!" Weston grins and pulls me as close as he

can with the center console between us. He presses a kiss to my temple. "Just watch."

That's when I see his two brothers, plus several other brutish football player types, all struggling to roll a large trash can across the parking lot. I know better than to ask. Ever since Weston picked me up this morning, he's been secretive and very excited.

I'm just glad he waited until he had already proposed to do this. Otherwise, I would have thought this was the engagement and been sorely disappointed by whatever this is.

Seth, Aaron, and their buddies get the trash can up over the lip of the sidewalk. Water sloshes out of the top, which makes me realize why they're having to struggle.

But why a trash can full of water?

They navigate the can right up to one of the apartment doors, and I start to get nervous. Carefully, they prop the can against the door, then all slowly remove their hands.

I'm beginning to see where this is going. An epic prank. But on whom? And why?

Weston is grinning. He senses me looking and squeezes my shoulder.

"This has been a long time coming. And is completely deserved. So, don't feel bad."

"Why would *I* feel bad? I'm just a passenger. I have no idea what's going on."

"Here we go!"

Weston points, and as we watch, Aaron gives Weston the thumbs up, and then knocks on the apartment door. Aaron and the rest of the big guys scatter, ducking behind cars and shrubbery until they're out of sight.

I throw a hand over my mouth, suddenly filled with nervous excitement for whatever this is.

The door opens. And like something out of a movie, things seem to slow down. The trash can tips, splashing water over the rim, and then falls to the ground.

A wave of water rolls out, even as the man standing in the doorway holds out his hands as if that could stop it. He's soaked in an instant as a trash can full of water rushes out and into his apartment.

A laugh bubbles out of me. "Weston! Why did you—"

A woman runs up to the door from inside the apartment. She's frantic while the man stands there like he can't believe that just happened.

I can't hear from where we sit, but it's clear she's screaming, her mouth open and her hands waving around. It all clicks into place when I recognize her. It's spider lashes, aka Melyssa, aka the girl Chad cheated on me with. I lean forward, squinting.

"It's Chad!" I breathe. "You're pranking Chad!"

"Yes. *We* are. And it's about time. I've been saving this—it's the longest I've ever waited."

I glance back once more at Chad and Melyssa, who have righted the trash can and are now using towels to sop up the water. Hope they've got a lot of towels.

I'm so surprised by this whole thing that it takes me a minute to decide how I feel. I don't harbor any weird feelings about seeing Chad still with Melyssa. I also realize that I don't feel guilty or bad at all about their current predicament. It's because I'm thinking about this that Weston's words sink in slowly.

I turn to him, grabbing his arm. "Wait. What do you mean the longest you've ever waited?"

Weston studies my face, biting back a smile. Clearly, he's trying to decide how much to tell me.

"West. Spill." I reach for the ticklish spot right on the side of his neck, and he laughs, trying to pull away. But in the front seat of the car, there's nowhere to go.

"Fine! Fine! I give."

I stop my tickle assault and lean back in my seat, waiting.

Weston runs a hand over his beard. "Let's just say that over the years, I've enjoyed making your exes pay for hurting you."

My eyes go wide. "You pranked my ex boyfriends? How many of them?"

Weston smirks. "All of them since tenth grade."

"You were the one who put fish in Wade's tailpipe? And the classified ad in the paper for Breck?"

"Yes and yes."

My mind is spinning. I didn't date that much, but there are probably eight guys I dated for at least a few months. I knew about the two pranks from high school but never would have guessed Weston was behind them.

It's … overwhelming. Because, like the stupid Christmas cheese ball, this is a totally strange and unexpected way Weston expressed his love for me. Totally ridiculous, obviously. I mean, who does stuff like this?

My fiancé. That's who.

"Are you mad?"

I guess I've been silent too long. I swing my face toward him, and he catches sight of my tears.

Immediately, his face softens. "Oh, hey. Don't cry. I'm sorry. I never should have—"

"No. I love it. I love you."

I launch myself across the car to press my mouth to his. Weston is surprised, but it only takes a moment for him to catch on. His hands sweep up my neck and tangle into my hair.

Our movements are hurried, filled with the kind of passion that comes from bottling up our feelings for so many years. It's been this way since Christmas, and for the past four months, we've been making up for lost time. To some, four months of dating and a six-month engagement would be way too fast.

But there's nothing I want more than this man. Every minute. Every day. I can't get enough.

I pour all of that into my kiss, letting my lips practice the vows I'm going to make. I cup my hands around his cheeks, stroking my fingers down his beard. The kiss slows, and I sigh against his mouth as we pull apart.

"I'm so glad you're mine, Weston. Finally."

"You don't think I'm terrible for pranking all your exes?"

I shake my head, laughing softly. "No. They were all such Chads. *Especially* Chad. I just have one question. A serious one."

"Lay it on me."

I run my fingers through his dark hair, meeting his caramel eyes with a smile.

"Since I won't have any more exes, who are we going to prank next?"

Slowly, sweetly, Weston's mouth meets mine in a kiss that has my heart doing a happy dance. When he pulls back, he grins, lips still grazing mine.

"I think now we both have better things to occupy our time than playing pranks," he says. "Would you agree?"

I brush my lips across his. "I do," I tell him.

I like the way that sounds, these words that I'll soon repeat in front of a church and our family and friends. Maybe in less than six months. That suddenly seems like much too long.

I meet Weston's eyes, again practicing the promise I can't wait to say for real. "I do."

Want more of Chase? You can read his story with Harper in *Falling for Your Best Friend!* Or turn the page to start a sample chapter…

CHAPTER ONE- FALLING FOR YOUR BEST FRIEND

Harper

No kid ever imagines that when they're an adult, filling out spreadsheets could bring as much joy as climbing a tree. Actually, I still love climbing trees. And rock walls and hills—anything really. As for being an adult, sometimes that only feels technically and legally true.

But watching the numbers—which I calculate first in my head—fill this color-coded Excel sheet brings with it a sense of satisfaction that I would never admit out loud. The sounds of weights clanging and bass thumping from the gym downstairs are blocked by my noise-canceling headphones, and I'm in a little bubble of happiness and peace.

Which, of course, can't last long. Movement drags my eyes from the screen, and I look up to see my brother Collin. In lieu of simply waving to get my attention, he's doing some kind of dorky dance—the funky chicken? Or the sprinkler? Dancing isn't my thing. It's not his either. Clearly.

If he weren't my brother, I might laugh, but since we're

CHAPTER ONE- FALLING FOR YOUR BEST FRIEND

related, I'm deeply embarrassed *for* and *by* him. Good thing we're alone in his office. The only window is a two-way mirror, so he can look down on the gym floor, but no one can see him. He likes to imagine himself like the Godfather up here.

I pull off my headphones and set them on the desk. They're a ridiculously expensive pair of baby-blue Beats, an early Christmas gift from my best friend, Chase. I really shouldn't have accepted them, since I know exactly how much they cost. But I couldn't say no. Not when I saw them in the box, and not when I saw the grin on Chase's face at my reaction. It was that rare smile, the one he saves just for me.

I'm not usually into material stuff. But they're functional, so pretty, and, as they say, it's the thought that counts. And every time I see them, I think of *him*. I got him the super-fancy mountain bike he's been drooling over, and I can't wait to give it to him Christmas morning.

"These are new," Collin says, picking them up and examining them. "Nice."

I fight back the urge to snatch them out of his hands. "Thanks."

His brows shoot up as he notices the logo. "Beats? Wow, sis. I didn't know you were so fancy."

"You know me. *So* fancy," I say, flipping my dark braid over one shoulder with an eye roll. He snorts.

I'm hoping Collin won't ask any more questions. I don't want him to know that Chase bought them for me. He'll take that totally the wrong way, then get that goofy, hopeful expression he and my two other brothers and even my dad get when it comes to my best guy friend. I'm constantly thwarting their hopes because Chase and I are, and will always be, *just friends*.

CHAPTER ONE- FALLING FOR YOUR BEST FRIEND

Their matchmaking schemes are irrelevant. Just like my actual feelings.

I retrieve my headphones and put them in their case before zipping them up in my gym bag. "So, what's up?"

"I wanted to check on the status of the spreadsheets," Collin says. "And remind you that you've got Kyle in ten minutes."

Just like that, all my spreadsheet-happy goes *poof*. Kyle. I hadn't forgotten my next training session, even if I kind of wanted to. Maybe I was using the number-crunching as a way of mentally preparing.

"Your financials are up to date for now," I tell Collin, sliding my palms up and down my thighs a few times, wishing the fabric could wick away my stress. "Merry Christmas."

"Aw, I'm not getting a real present?" Collin sticks out his lip and blinks his big brown eyes at me. From an objective standpoint, all my brothers are stupidly good-looking. This puppy-dog face could slay about any woman in the Austin area. Doesn't work on sisters, though.

"I figured free accounting for your gym is a pretty solid present." When he opens his mouth, I hold up both hands. "Kidding. You know I like doing it."

"But I could pay you extra—"

"Nope."

And I'm not just saying it because I know how close his profit margins are. Sure, Grit charges a premium for collegiate athletes like Kyle and even some pros. Our family name carries weight, even long after my dad and two of my three brothers retired from football. But the gym costs a premium to run as well. High-end clients require high-end equipment and trainers. Grit is only in its second year, a baby business that's just moving into the black. The last thing Collin would

CHAPTER ONE- FALLING FOR YOUR BEST FRIEND

want is to have to ask Dad for a bailout. Dad's already done enough by investing and endorsing the gym.

Before the knee injury that finally took him out, my dad was a defensive end, playing for Tennessee and Dallas. He and Mom loved Texas and decided to settle in Austin to raise my three brothers and me once he retired. A year later, Mom died of cancer, so Dad raised the four of us alone.

Which explains some of why I am the way I am. The only girl in a house full of testosterone-fueled guys? I was bound to be a little wonky.

Anyway, even if I weren't personally invested in wanting to see Collin succeed, I actually *like* doing the spreadsheets, almost as much and sometimes more than I do training. Especially when it comes to guys like Kyle.

Not that he's done anything bad … yet. Today is our second session, and during our first, I got a vibe. Nothing I could pinpoint exactly. Like a lot of athletes who spend time in the spotlight, he's got an ego that stretches on for miles. One I'd personally like to knock down a peg or ten.

Maybe in our first session he stood a little too close and seemed to look a little too long. I don't think he was flirty, though I sometimes miss innuendo and jokes. My roommate, Abby, is forever having to explain things to me, laughing at what she likes to call my virginal ears.

Kyle is probably fine. Ninety-nine percent of the time, I'm the issue if things are weird, in and out of the gym. Whenever I start with new clients, I'm a bit stiff. I have an adjustable script in my head, and I focus as completely as possible on the tasks, the reps, the weights. Not so much the *person*. Once I'm used to a person, it's fine. More than fine, considering the fact that my schedule rarely opens up for new clients.

"So, you're good with Kyle?" Collin asks, and I realize my

CHAPTER ONE- FALLING FOR YOUR BEST FRIEND

worry must have shown on my face. "It could be a big deal if he endorses us. A few social media posts could do us good. But it's not worth it if he's—"

"Fine," I say, hoping to convince myself as well. Kyle is what Collin would call a whale—a great athlete with a solid social media presence. He basically *is* the University of Texas defense, at least until he gets snapped up by some pro team.

"Are you sure?"

Collin gives me a look that I don't like, but one I'm used to getting from any one of my three older brothers. I use the same one on my best friends, who are much more scared of my bark than I am of Collin's bite. I meet and hold his dark gaze that mirrors my own.

Once, Chase told me that my eyes are the color of the sun shining through a bottle of Dr Pepper. I don't even drink soda, but the specificity of that comparison made my chest tight. In a good way, not like the current stressful pinch I'm trying to hide from my brother.

"I can handle Kyle," I tell Collin, my voice sounding more confident than I feel. "And I know you'll be watching from your ivory tower, princess." I point to the window.

Collin rolls his eyes. "I've told you. When I'm up here, looking down on y'all, think of me as the Godfather."

He makes a face that I think is supposed to resemble Marlon Brando. Really, he just looks constipated.

I laugh and head for the door. "Sure thing, princess."

"You and Chase are coming to dinner, right?" he calls as I start down the stairs, my bag on my shoulder.

"It's Tuesday, isn't it?" I call back. Ever since I basically forced my family to adopt Chase, he's only missed a handful of our Tuesday dinners.

Collin snorts some kind of response and slams his office door. I make my way to the bank of treadmills and pull my

97

CHAPTER ONE- FALLING FOR YOUR BEST FRIEND

headphones out of my bag. I have a few minutes before Kyle shows up. A few sprints should give me a nice buzz of endorphins and a clearer head.

The best thing about Chase's gift is that the headphones can play music or simply cancel background noise. Right now, I need to borrow someone else's strength, so I locate Chase's Pump Up the Jam playlist, an upbeat mix of '80s, '90s, and early 2000s pop and rock. As MC Hammer starts in on being too legit, I begin a set of quick sprints.

You'll handle Kyle. The session will be fine. You'll be professional, not awkward or weird, and he'll tell all his friends about Grit, and Collin's profit margins will get a little more wiggle room.

As my feet pound on the belt, legs pumping, I repeat these things over and over again until the words are as familiar as my heartbeat: *You'll be fine. Everything will be fine.*

———

"Another," I say, my hands resting lightly on the bar holding 350 pounds above Kyle's chest. "I know you have at least one more rep in you."

Kyle doesn't curse, but I can see the urge to do so in his narrowed eyes. Even if he wants to, he doesn't have the breath for any words right now. He's using all his oxygen to push his body to its limit. And even though I don't want to be and won't show that I'm impressed, I am. I still feel like there's a weird vibe, but Kyle's physical capabilities are impressive, and he's giving it everything he has.

"Now," I snap. And then, because I know what motivates men like Kyle, I say, "Philip Cartwright did two more reps. Same amount of weight. Yesterday."

A new look flashes in Kyle's eyes and it's a thing of

CHAPTER ONE - FALLING FOR YOUR BEST FRIEND

beauty when he lifts the bar not one more time, not two, but three, just so he can beat Philip Cartwright's record.

Or what I *told* him was the record.

"Good," I say as he drops the bar back in place. More than good, but *good* is what he gets. In these early sessions, I'm serious and intense, saying only what I need to. People usually see it as being focused, not that I'm covering for being uncomfortable around new people.

I try not to flinch at the clang of metal on metal as the bar drops. It's a sound I should be used to, but it still gets to me, making me suddenly aware of all the noises in the room. Nearby, someone else lets weights fall with a thud. The low music playing switches to a faster tempo. I hear laughter, snatches of conversation, and the receptionist answering the phone out front. My breathing picks up, and I hear that too.

Focus, I remind myself, bringing my gaze back to Kyle, who is watching me. Shifting my attention helps the background noise stay where it should.

Kyle rises to his full height, his bronze skin gleaming with sweat, veins popping, muscles twitching. If I were skilled at art, I would be a sculptor, not a personal trainer. There's just something objectively beautiful about the human body in peak physical condition.

I could totally see myself spending all day, every day alone in a studio, chiseling muscles out of stone. Feeling the smooth marble under my fingers. I guess that kind of is what I do, just with a different medium—actual human beings.

"Dang, girl. You don't play," Kyle says, breathing heavy and giving me an appraising look, as though he's just started to understand me.

I bristle internally at being called *girl*, but it doesn't so much as ripple my cool exterior. "You don't pay me to play.

CHAPTER ONE- FALLING FOR YOUR BEST FRIEND

You pay me to help you get more time on the field. Is it working?"

His grin is cocky. "Don't tell me you didn't watch the game?"

"Which game?"

Of course, I watched the game. UT creamed LSU, with Kyle making two sacks and a few other key plays. But he doesn't need to know that. It would only fuel his ego, which has all the hot air of the Hindenburg.

Ego makes my job harder. You can't train someone who doesn't think they need training. Unless you can find the pain points of that ego and jab at them. It takes a delicate hand. Push too hard, and those guys tend to lash out. Feed it, and they get fat and lazy.

I like to think of myself as the Gordon Ramsay of the gym. People don't hire me because I smile and act like their cheerleader, passing out praise and high fives like candy. They hire me because they need to be *pushed*. I happen to like pushing. Pushing myself, pushing other people. I've never met a limit I liked.

"You don't watch your clients?" he asks, taking a quick drink. His eyes never leave me.

"I have a lot of clients."

I don't want Kyle to think I have any interest in him—his gameplay or otherwise—outside of my brother's gym. The only way this job works for me, especially as a woman in a male-dominated space, is keeping boundaries. Lots of them.

They are my moat. I like to imagine it teeming with hungry crocodiles.

Kyle's eyes narrow. "Was that Philip Cartwright thing even true?"

I shrug. "I don't share details of my clients' sessions."

Kyle's mouth pops open, and for a moment, I think he's

CHAPTER ONE- FALLING FOR YOUR BEST FRIEND

angry. He wouldn't be the first athlete to have a temper. I tense but remind myself that he and I aren't alone at Grit. And that Collin is likely doing that Godfather thing up there. He would be on Kyle in two seconds if he needed to be.

Finally, Kyle cracks a smile, the kind that probably has college girls tossing their panties at him. It does nothing for me.

"I wasn't sure why everyone said you were the one to work with. A little thing like you."

I may be a foot shorter than Kyle, but I'm no little thing. Often, I run or lift or jump right alongside my clients, depending on who it is and what we're doing.

But I feel small as Kyle looks me up and down. I can feel his eyeballs like little ants crawling over my skin. He removes two of the plates from the bar, and I realize too late that I'm standing next to where he needs to re-rack the weights. The wall is at my back, leaving no escape as Kyle steps closer.

I press back against the wall, running my palms over my legs until I realize I'm doing it. I shove my hands behind my back, feeling the scrape of the cinder-block on my fingertips. Kyle's body is so close that he ruffles the hem of my loose tank top. The way he's angled his body means that I can't get by to step away. Not without vaulting over the equipment in front of me.

He turns back to me after putting the plate away, his hands coiled into fists at his sides. Our chests are nearly brushing. I almost wish he'd say something that crosses the line. If he touched me, he would be officially violating gym policy, which restricts touching to fist bumps and anything necessary for a particular exercise. It's not enforced often, but Collin would if he needed to. If I needed him to.

But Kyle doesn't touch me. He simply invades my personal space, something ugly and alive crackling in the air

CHAPTER ONE- FALLING FOR YOUR BEST FRIEND

between us. I try to keep my breaths steady, focusing on my diaphragm as I breathe in for four, out for four.

Keep it together, Harper. Breathe. I can't meet his eyes, so I fix my gaze on his shoulder instead.

"This *little thing* has another session now. If you want to get on my regular rotation, talk to Jenna at the front desk. It's up to you if you want to see three or four sacks, not just two, in your next game."

I'm proud of myself. My voice sounds even, revealing none of the discomfort I feel. I even nudged at that ego a bit, pushing for a reaction. Anything to make him step away.

Kyle blinks and steps back. The air whooshes out of my lungs, but I keep my face blank. Whatever expression he had has been replaced with shock. I've stunned him, this man who is more shredded than paperwork at a crooked company about to get audited.

He laughs, head back and throat bobbing, slick with sweat. The body that I was just admiring for its peak physical condition now seems intimidating. But poking at that ego seems to be working for me, so I'll stick with that.

You've got this. And now that I'm not trapped against the wall by that wall of muscle, I feel more at ease.

"Girl, can I trust anything you say?"

"You can trust me with your body."

The words were meant to sound tough, but instantly, I realize my mistake. Instead, they sounded like flirting. An invitation. I swallow.

Kyle's eyes change from laughing to … something else, darker and more heated. I swear, pheromones are coming off him in a cloud. He licks his lips, but as he's about to step closer, I brush by him, hitting my hip on the weight rack as I go.

I don't even mind the sting of it, because I have space to

CHAPTER ONE- FALLING FOR YOUR BEST FRIEND

move. Kyle doesn't have me cornered. I told Collin I could handle this. I can.

Stick to the script, I remind myself. *Weights. Reps. Push. Don't branch out into funny or sarcastic. You're not Abby or Sam. Breathe.*

And this is one of the many reasons I try to keep to a loose script. I can't even trust myself to not flirt or make accidental innuendos, to give a green light when what I'd rather do is to raise up my drawbridge.

I cross my arms. You stand your ground with most predators and try to make yourself look bigger.

Kyle's smile is feral. "How would you like to—"

"Harper!"

Something in my chest loosens and unfurls at the sound of Chase calling my name. I'm happy any time he's around, but at this moment, I could kiss him. Figuratively speaking, of course. Actually kissing him? Not going to happen.

"Are you almost ready?" Chase asks as he reaches us.

I can see the way his eyes scan my face and body language in half a second. If anyone could read my discomfort or panic, it would be Chase. I try to look as calm as I can. *Nothing wrong here. I'm just fine.*

He doesn't believe that for a second, and steps between me and Kyle, sticking out his hand. "Hey, man," he says in a casual tone.

But I know him at least as well as he thinks he knows me, and I can hear the restraint in his tone. Also, the warning. Kyle shakes his hand, and I don't miss the slight wince. Chase may not be as big as Kyle, but he's all muscle. He was actually my first client, before I officially took clients. Those abs, hidden under his shirt? Those shoulders? That flexing forearm? Yeah, I helped build that.

"I'm Chase. Great game Saturday."

CHAPTER ONE- FALLING FOR YOUR BEST FRIEND

"Thanks, man." Kyle drops his hand and flicks his gaze back to me.

I shift my weight closer to Chase. I don't want to be some princess needing rescue, but his presence is comforting and steady. The threat of Kyle—real or imagined—has been dissolved.

It takes me only a moment to locate the words I need to close out our session. "Decent work today, Kyle. You could do better. But it wasn't bad."

Kyle chuckles, shaking his head at me. "You're something else."

I step forward and hold out my hand for a fist bump. That's the gym's policy, and it was before I came on staff, so I know it's not a concession Collin made for me because I hate being touched by people I'm not close to.

But Kyle bypasses the fist bump and, for the second time today, invades my space. Before I can duck out of it, he is wrapping his arms around me, yanking me close in a possessive move that has all my internal alarms going off.

I shudder, struggling away from his slick body. The heat of it, the hardness, the unfamiliarity. My cheek is plastered to his shirt. The scent of his deodorant fills my nostrils, and I can't breathe. The room is suddenly too hot, too loud, every sound converging into a discordant symphony.

Kyle's arms are like the shoulder harness of a roller coaster, locked and lowered into place. I want off the ride.

I can feel Kyle everywhere now, his touch spreading like a virus over my skin. I know rationally it's only been a few seconds, but they have stretched out to feel like half my life.

And then he's ripped away from me. When I can open my eyes again, Chase is on one side of him, my brother on the other, each holding one of Kyle's muscled arms. I try to breathe steadily, not to show the panic and disgust on my

CHAPTER ONE- FALLING FOR YOUR BEST FRIEND

face. I'm biting the inside of my cheek, my palms skating over my thighs again and again.

More than I hate his touch, I hate that I react this way. It shouldn't be a big deal. I should shake it off and remind him of the gym policy. But I can still feel him all over me, and I know I won't shake this feeling for hours.

"Leave," Collin says simply, but with enough force that Kyle only half-heartedly argues as he tries to break free of their grips.

"Come on, man. It was just a hug."

"She didn't ask for a hug." Chase's eyes bleed fire.

As much as I hate being rescued or being talked about like I'm not here, Chase has never been sexier than he is in this moment. Too bad I can't enjoy it, because the feel of Kyle is on me like a full-body tattoo. I want to peel off my skin and leave it here on the rubber mat.

Kyle scoffs. "It's a hug. If you start talking to me about consent—"

Collin sneers. "It's Grit *policy*. One which was made very clear to you when you walked through the doors and spoke to me personally. You signed off on it. Outside of fist bumps or physical contact necessary for the exercise at hand, no touching. Now, let's go."

This scene hasn't escaped the notice of the rest of the gym. Even though this is a safe spot for me, one where I'm respected if not somewhat revered because of my family and my own reputation, I don't like this kind of attention. I'm too bothered by the itching of my skin to be properly humiliated, though I know I will be later when I replay this moment in my mind, again and again. What I could have done differently. What I could have said differently. How many ways I messed up from the start of the session until the end.

As my brother hauls Kyle toward the door, flanked by

CHAPTER ONE- FALLING FOR YOUR BEST FRIEND

another staff member, Chase steps in front of me, catching my attention without touching me. Though I wish he would. Honestly, after unwanted contact like that, what I really want is the safety of Chase's arms.

"How about a run?" Chase asks, and I'm already nodding, my skin yearning for a release, to sweat off anything left of Kyle.

It will be hours still before my skin quiets, until the buzz stops where Kyle touched me. Running will help. So will a super-hot shower, where I can wash and rinse, then repeat. But only time will fully erase the sting of it in my skin.

As we step out into the unseasonably warm December afternoon, I focus on Chase's comforting presence. His footfalls, his breathing, the swing of his arms. Having his warm body close to mine is like the ultimate tease. Because he makes me so happy, happier than I've ever been, even after something like Kyle.

It's a stark reminder that Chase deserves someone who does the same for him. Someone who doesn't need so much, who doesn't require so much consideration. Someone who is normal, not just pretending to be.

ALSO BY EMMA ST. CLAIR

Love Clichés
Falling for Your Best Friend's Twin
Falling for Your Boss
Falling for Your Fake Fiancé
The Twelve Holidates
Falling for Your Best Friend
Falling for Your Enemy

Hometown Heartthrob Series
Marrying Her Dream Groom
Forgiving Her First Love
Loving Her Cowboy
Trusting Her Cowboy Poet
Managing the Rock Star

The Billionaire Surprise Series
The Billionaire Love Match
The Billionaire Benefactor
The Billionaire Land Baron
The Billionaire's Masquerade Ball
The Billionaire's Secret Heir

Sandover Island Sweet Romance Series
Sandover Beach Memories
Sandover Beach Week
Sandover Beach Memories

Sandover Beach Christmas

Sandover Beach Series
Secrets Whispered from the Sea

A NOTE FROM EMMA

In late 2020, I debated trying to write a Christmas novella. I promptly decided I had TOO MANY other book projects happening!

Then I saw the original cover, from Sharon at Book Cover Bug, and I had an idea to write a short novella that loosely tied into the romcom series where I've been focused.

Best idea ever!

(I later changed the cover to fit in with the series.)

It was a little weird because time-wise, this book takes place after book three (*Falling for Your Fake Fiancé*), but I wrote it BEFORE.

Then when writing book four (*Falling for Your Best Friend*), I had to revisit this a lot, since Taylor's date with Chase is part of that storyline.

I had SO MUCH FUN writing this one, which I did mostly from the passenger seat while on a trip with my husband this December. We drove around Texas and I'd type on my phone, then read it out loud to him.

How romantic, right?!

A NOTE FROM EMMA

Because it was SUCH a quick turnaround, the editing process was a bit more lax than usual. A HUGE thank you to Devon, Teresa, Marti, Sharon, Priscilla, Lyn, and Marsha for being my eyes. *(A few of you might have also read but emailed after I finished—so thankful for you too!!)*

I'm super thankful for all of my loyal readers and to my cheerleaders who keep me going.

This series has been my favorite to write! I feel totally immersed in the characters, and even these side characters like Weston and Taylor. If you liked Chase, don't miss *Falling for Your Best Friend*.

You can reach out via email, but I'll warn you my inbox is a pit of death: emma@emmastclair.com

Thanks for reading! If you enjoyed this, leave a review and/or tell a friend!

-emma

Emma St. Clair is a *USA Today* bestselling author of over twenty books. She loves sweet love stories and characters with a lot of sass. Her stories range from rom-com to women's fiction and all will have humor, heart, and nothing that's going to make you need to hide your Kindle from the kids. ;)

Sign up for her romcom emails: http://emmastclair.com/romcomemail

Or join her reader group at https://www.facebook.com/groups/emmastclair/

Connect on Instagram: https://instagram.com/kikimojo